Death
by Fire

Also by Hugh Pentecost

Uncle George Mystery Novels

MURDER SWEET AND SOUR
THE PRICE OF SILENCE
THE COPYCAT KILLERS
CHOICE OF VIOLENCE

Death by Fire

An Uncle George Mystery Novel

Hugh Pentecost

DODD, MEAD & COMPANY
NEW YORK

Copyright © 1986 by Judson Philips
All rights reserved
No part of this book may be reproduced in any form
without permission in writing from the publisher.
Published by Dodd, Mead & Company, Inc.
79 Madison Avenue, New York, N.Y. 10016
Distributed in Canada by
McClelland and Stewart Limited, Toronto
Manufactured in the United States of America
First Edition

1 2 3 4 5 6 7 8 9 10

Library of Congress Cataloging-in-Publication Data

Pentecost, Hugh.
    Death by fire.

    I. Title.
PS3531.H442D38   1986   813'.52   86-8907
ISBN 0-396-08826-0

Death
by Fire

Part One

1

The tragedy and what the local newspaper called "a holocaust" struck the small New England town of Lakeview on a summer night in June. Fire broke out at the Seth Harder dairy farm at the north end of town just before midnight. The barns and the house were both engulfed in flames, and Seth Harder, a well-liked local man, born and raised in the town, was trapped under fallen beams in the barn where he was trying to rescue some of his livestock, and died there while his young daughter and her two-year-old son watched helplessly.

Fire in a small town activates most of the able-bodied citizens. The men are members of the local volunteer fire department, the women are ready to help the injured, get them to the hospital, provide them with shelter or, at the least, comfort.

The fire at the Harder farm had most of those able-bodied men and women on hand to help, shocked by the total disaster to a neighbor and friend. In the midst of that fight for life and property the fire siren sounded again. There was a second fire somewhere in town. A portable phone informed the local fire chief that this second blaze was at the Town Hall in the very center of Lakeview, a couple of miles away. No equipment could be spared, and help was asked for from surrounding towns. Half a dozen firemen left the Harder disaster and headed for the second blaze. There were not likely to be any lives involved in the Town Hall building at that time of night, but of course there would be danger to the homes and businesses that adjoined it. The fire fighters who left the Harder disaster were concerned with their own personal properties that might be threatened.

When the sun rose the next morning, the town of Lakeview was shadowed by clouds of dark smoke that still hovered overhead. The people couldn't believe what had happened in their lovely, peaceful town. The Harder farm was gone, and Seth Harder was dead. The Town Hall had consisted of two two-story buildings connected by a center section, shaped like a giant letter H with an excessively wide crossbar. All three sections had burned to the ground, destroying two hundred years' worth of town records and historical momentos. Neither those records nor the building with its graceful white pillars fronting the main street could ever be replaced. By some miracle no serious damage was done to any neighboring structures. Thank God there had been no wind.

One word was on all the lips in town that morning: Arson!

"You pay your money and you take your chance," George Crowder said to his friend Red Egan, the local sheriff. The two men, looking exhausted, eyes reddened by smoke, were having coffee in the lunchroom across the street from the ashes of the Town Hall, which was still smoking.

"Either the Harder place was torched to make sure there was no one to fight the fire here in town, or the Town Hall was torched to drag people away from Seth Harder's farm to make certain that disaster would be total."

"Or we're dealing with a psycho who enjoys watching fires and may well set a couple more tonight."

"Not if half the town is out watching for him," George Crowder said. "And we will be!"

Newcomers to the town of Lakeview would probably

4

have referred to George Crowder as a "character." Gray-haired, a rather distinguished-looking man in his early fifties, Crowder lived alone in a log cabin he'd built for himself on Lakeview Mountain with no company except his setter dog, Timmy. Born and raised in Lakeview, Crowder had gone on to college and law school, set up a practice for himself in Lakeview, and eventually had been elected County Attorney. As the official prosecutor, he had tried a man for murder, gotten his conviction, and seen the guilty man executed by the state. Then, far too late, fresh evidence was revealed that indicated that the wrong man had paid for the crime. George Crowder resigned his post as County Attorney, closed his law office, and disappeared. Not even his sister, Esther, married to the town's druggist, knew where her brother had gone. Rumor had it that he was drinking himself to death somewhere. Then one day, ten years after his disappearance, George Crowder returned to Lakeview, built himself his cabin on the mountain, and appeared to be perfectly sound of mind and body. He never told anyone how he had used those ten missing years.

Esther Trimble, Crowder's sister, had a son, Joey, born only a couple of years before Crowder's troubles. Now Joey worshiped his newly discovered uncle. He let the world know. "My Uncle George is the greatest man in the whole state with a rifle or shotgun. My Uncle George is the best trout fisherman you ever saw! My Uncle George is the greatest man with hunting dogs in the whole state, maybe in the whole world! My Uncle George—"

So the eulogy went, and in time most of Crowder's friends and acquaintances came to call him "Uncle George." He was liked and respected by the older people in town for his worldly wisdom, his kindness and help for people in trouble. The younger people admired him for his skills as a hunter, a fisherman, and for his special abilities as a woodsman. They also liked him because he didn't treat them as irresponsible kids, but as equals.

"You have many arson cases when you were the D.A., George?" Red Egan asked his friend.

Uncle George shook his head, slowly. "Only one that I can remember—the old Telford lumberyard about fifteen years ago."

"I remember. Some workman who got fired."

"Arson is very hard to prove," Uncle George said. "State Police presented me with half a dozen cases in my time, but there wasn't enough evidence to justify a trial. It's a hard crime to prove. I remember seeing figures some-where. Only about two percent of suspected arsons ever result in a conviction."

"Evidence destroyed in the fire itself," Red Egan said.

"That, and in a sick mind somewhere. No way to get at that unless you're super lucky."

Red Egan, who was facing the window to the street, indulged in a tight little smile. "Looks like your press agent is headed this way, George."

"Joey?" Uncle George turned and saw his young nephew, Joey Trimble, headed toward the lunchroom.

"Looks like he lost his best friend. Didn't I see him out at the Harder fire?"

Uncle George wasn't smiling. "Damn near buried in that burning barn along with Seth Harder. He was trying to be a hero and I just did manage to drag him out. No way Seth could have been saved, but the boy was trying."

"Great kid."

"Ruby Harder was his fifth-grade teacher," Uncle George said. "His first passionate love affair. I guess he'd risk anything for her."

Joey Trimble, a fair-haired, blue-eyed boy of thirteen, was well liked by the adults in the community. Not a troublemaker, and he was partly a Crowder—Esther's son

6

and George's nephew. Had he taken after his father, Hector
Trimble, he might not have rated so high. Hector, a first-
rate pharmacist and drugstore operator, was an arbitrary,
always-right man who chose to sit in judgment on everyone
in the world except himself. There had been a time when it
had been assumed that Esther Crowder would marry her
recognized boyfriend in her college years, Red Egan. She
returned from college after her senior year with a husband,
Hector Trimble. It was a choice no one could understand.

Joey came into the lunchroom, looking tired and misera-
ble.

"I saw your Jeep out front," he said to Uncle George. He
tried smiling at Red Egan but it was a poor imitation of his
usual grin. "I guess some of us got lucky."

"Meaning?" Uncle George asked.

"My dad says it's a miracle that more homes and businesses weren't caught up in the Town Hall fire."

"No wind," Red Egan said. "If there'd been wind, a
whole block of homes and businesses might have gone,
including your father's house and drugstore."

Joey looked at his uncle. "If anyone saw anything that
might lead to the person who set the fires, they should go
to the State Police, shouldn't they?"

"On the double," Uncle George said.

"My dad says that unless you saw someone actually
doing something, can name him, you'll just be inviting
trouble. Your house, your business, could be marked down
for the next fire."

"You saw something or someone, Joey?" Uncle George
asked.

"No!" Joey said, quickly.

"Then what's the problem?"

"It's just that Dad says you shouldn't tell anyone what
you saw unless the cops can make an arrest."

"He saw something?"

7

"If he did, he wouldn't tell us," Joey said.

"So who do you think did see something?" Red Egan asked. "Everybody in town thinks they saw something, or suspects something."

"I know," Joey said. "But if someone saw something that made it certain it wasn't Fletch Johnson who set the Town Hall fire—"

"Fletch Johnson?"

"A lot of people are saying that Fletch Johnson set the fire at the Harders' farm because Mr. Harder fired him. Miss Ruby says that's absurd, crazy. But if I saw someone else who set the Town Hall fire that couldn't be Fletch Johnson—"

Seth Harder's life had been marked by tragedy for a quarter of a century and had ended in violent death and the loss of his major battle, a fight to keep his dairy farm alive in a sea of debts. His first tragedy, twenty-five years ago, had been the loss of his wife while she was giving birth to his daughter, Ruby. Raising a child without a mother to help can be quite a chore for a man who works sixteen hours a day. Neighboring women tried to help, as did teachers when Ruby got to be school age, but even that isn't enough. Ruby did well though, school and college and then a teaching job in Lakeview's elementary school. When it was announced that she was going to marry Bradley Smith, a well-thought-of young man from the next town, people were happy for her. There was talk of what a good job Seth Harder had done raising a girl child without a woman to share the responsibility.

And then a double tragedy struck at Seth Harder again. On the way to the wedding, which was to be held at the Harder farm, young Bradley Smith's car was struck by a trailer truck, smashed into a tree, and the bridegroom was killed before he ever got to say the vows. Sad for Harder and tragic for Ruby. And then Harder got it right between

8

the eyes. Ruby was pregnant. No one doubted that the unfortunate bridegroom was the father—a little prenuptial hanky-panky. For Seth Harder, a deacon of the church, abortion was just not in his creed. He felt no pleasure in the prospect of becoming a grandfather, only shame that the whole world would know that his daughter was "a loose woman."

And so Ruby Harder had a baby, a little boy. Since Ruby had no married name, he was called Rodney Harder, the Rodney after Seth's father. Ruby had been fired from her job as a teacher as soon as it was obvious that she was going to have a baby, and she and young Rod became totally dependent on Seth, who ruled the roost with an iron fist. Ruby was transformed from a treasured daughter into an enslaved house servant. Little Rod, a visible symbol of the Harder shame, was almost hidden away from neighbors and farm workers.

The Fletcher Johnson story had become a juicy bit of local gossip a few weeks back. Johnson, an out-of-towner, had found himself a job at the Harder farm some months ago. He was a big, tall, handsome young man in his late twenties. A couple of weeks ago Seth Harder and another of his hands, a local boy named Dave Williams, had gone to the farmhouse in mid-afternoon to get a special tool that was needed to fix a piece of farm machinery. Unexpected, they walked in on Ruby locked in a passionate embrace with Fletcher Johnson. The story of what followed was spread by Dave Williams, an eyewitness.

"Seth let out a shout that split Ruby and Fletch apart as though they'd been struck by lightning," was the way Dave told it. "Seth, at the top of his lungs, shouted, 'Having a whore for a daughter, I should have expected something like this!' 'Keep your filthy mouth off Ruby, you old jerk!' Fletch shouted back. Then Seth headed for the rifle that hung over the mantel at the fireplace. He grabbed it down and swung

9

it around toward Fletch. 'You're fired!' he yelled. 'Get out of my house, get out of this town! You show your ugly face again, anywhere, and I'll blow your head off!' Then Ruby ran to Seth and tried to push the gun away so it wasn't pointing at Fletch. Seth struck her across the mouth, so hard that it knocked her flat on her fanny. I could see blood trickling down her chin. Fletch started forward to help her and Seth stuck the rifle barrel right in his gut. 'Out, if you want to stay alive!' Seth said. They stood facing each other and I guess Fletch knew that Seth meant what he said. But he had his say before he turned and left. 'You'll pay for this, old man. Not for not liking me, but for hitting Ruby. You'll pay for it in spades, if it's the last thing I ever do on this earth.'"

The town had been chewing on this delicious morsel for a couple of weeks and now it appeared to most of them that Fletch Johnson had carried out his threat "in spades." But why the Town Hall?

"I saw Fletch up there at the Harder farm fighting the fire," Uncle George said.

"Perfect way to cover himself, wouldn't you say?" Red asked. "Anyway, Jim Purdy's arrested him and is questioning him." Captain Purdy is in command of the local State Police barracks.

"But if someone saw someone who couldn't have been Fletch Johnson—?" Joey said.

Uncle George pushed back his chair. "I think you and I should go talk to your folks, boy," he said.

Joey trotted toward the door. It appeared that that was what he'd wanted all along.

Esther Crowder Trimble, approaching forty, was a handsome woman in a nonglamorous way. Nothing could ruffle her feathers, not even her husband's "know-better-than-anyone-else" approach to their daily lives. People still wondered how Hector Trimble, thin, tight-lipped, with a little military mustache decorating his upper lip and pale, cold blue eyes protected by steel-rimmed glasses, had ever persuaded Esther that he was her man.

Uncle George was aware as soon as he and Joey walked into the Trimble house that there were storm clouds still hanging overhead. Esther was rather too vigorously polishing silver, and Hector, like a comic version of Horatio at the bridge, hands locked behind his back, was waiting for the attack.

"I suppose he told you," Hector said to Uncle George, indicating Joey.

"Told me what, Hector?"

"What I told him not to tell."

"He asked me a hypothetical question," Uncle George said.

"And, as usual, you gave him a hypothetical answer," Hector said. "What one of your fictional heroes would do!" He resented the fact that Uncle George had influenced a lot of Joey's reading. Romantic trash, he called it.

"I asked Uncle George a legal question because he's a lawyer," Joey said.

"A lawyer who hasn't practiced law for years is not my idea of the best source for a legal opinion," Hector said.

"Oh, Hector!" Esther dropped a silver fork on the floor. Well, anyway, she hadn't thrown it, Uncle George thought.

"You want to tell me what it is one of you saw?" Uncle George asked. "If not, I'll be off. It's been a strenuous night and morning."

"What was seen was really nothing," Hector said.

"Then why can't it be told?"

"Because we're dealing with some kind of a maniac," Hector said. "If he hears that Esther saw him but hasn't

11

identified him yet, we may be the next family to go under the torch in time to stop her. That's the way that kind of sick mind works."

"You want to tell me what you saw, Es?" Uncle George asked.

"I've been forbidden by Hector to tell anyone."

"Did you know they've arrested Fletcher Johnson for possibly setting the Harder fire?"

"No," Esther said.

"But that sounds right on target," Hector said.

"Could the person you saw have been Fletch Johnson?" Uncle George asked his sister.

"You might as well tell him," Hector said. "It'll be all over town now that you saw something."

"We were all awakened by the siren around eleven," Esther said. "Hector took off to check with the ambulance corps. They might need things at the store. Joey headed for the Harders when he heard where the fire was." She smiled at the boy. "His Miss Ruby."

Joey avoided his uncle's questioning look.

"I started making a picnic-size pot of coffee," Esther went on. "When there's an emergency like this, people are always wanting coffee. Just as I was pouring water into the pot I heard an explosion out front. Sounded like a car backfiring, or maybe a big truck. What seemed like only a few seconds later, there was a second backfire. Then I saw some kind of flickering light against my kitchen window. I went to the window. I was shocked by what I saw. The north wing and the center section of the Town Hall were blazing, as though they'd been burning for hours and just reached a peak."

"Some kind of fire bombs," Uncle George said.

"Then, as I was standing there, too shocked to go to the phone, I heard the siren. Someone else had turned in the alarm. And then—the third explosion. It—it was the

12

darnedest thing, George. The south wing was a ball of fire. No starting point, no gradual growing—the full works all at once!"

"That will help confirm the theory of fire bombs already being discussed by the firemen and the cops," Uncle George said. "But I got the impression you saw someone."

Esther nodded slowly. "A boy, running out of the south wing just a moment after the bomb went off there," Esther said.

"Can you describe him?"

"I only saw his back. He was running away."

"Fletch Johnson is a big man, well over six feet, broad shoulders," Joey interrupted. "Mom says—"

"Let her tell it, Joey," Uncle George said.

"This wasn't a big man," Esther said. "A boy, small, agile, running like a deer."

"More details?"

"Dark hair, worn longish."

"As most of the boys do today," Hector said. His tone of voice told what his attitude was toward today's long-haired young people.

"Anything else?" Uncle George asked.

"Dark pants, could have been blue jeans," Esther said. "A dark shirt—blue or black. He just raced around the corner and was gone, almost before I had a chance to focus on him."

"You wouldn't know him if you saw him again?"

"I don't think so, George. Dozens of young boys in town look like what I saw."

"So she didn't see anything," Hector said. "She shouldn't tell what she didn't see. That creep, whoever he is, thinks he's safe. If he hears Esther saw someone he'll suspect she saw more than she did. A maniac like that would put us at the top of his list. If Esther could really nail him—"

"Her account of the three explosions will help make the fire bomb theory a solid one," Uncle George said.

"But leave out the kid," Hector said.

"But if the police think it's Fletch Johnson," Joey said, "then what Mom saw will make them look somewhere else."

"Is there any law that says the same man must have set both fires?" Hector asked. "Everyone knows Fletch Johnson intended to get even with Seth Harder."

Uncle George tugged at his lower lip. "One thing's for sure," he said. "Fire bombs don't grow on trees. They'd have to be bought or made, and making them isn't something a kid could do without special equipment and special skills. Three bombs? That suggests careful preparation to set a special fire involving a special building."

"Why would Fletcher Johnson want to blow up the Town Hall?" Esther asked. "What would that have to do with his feud with Seth Harder?"

"Good question," Uncle George said. "I'd like to tell Ben Bowers, the fire chief, and Captain Purdy of the State Police, that you heard those three explosions, Es, and saw a kid running away—a kid you couldn't identify if you saw him again."

"And if I say no you'll do it anyway," Hector said.

"Not to spite you, Hector, but to catch a murderer. Seth Harder is dead, and a dangerous mental case is on the loose, ready to strike again."

"At us, at me and my family," Hector said, "if you blab!"

We live in a world of specialists, Uncle George told himself as he walked out of Hector's house and onto the main street, where townspeople were gathered to stare at the ruins of their historic Town Hall. The State Police have specialists in homicide, specialists in car thefts, specialists in vandalism, specialists in arson. No one intelligent, well-

14

trained man even attempts to handle all the problems in these times.

The still-smoking ashes of the Town Hall were too hot for any kind of search of the wreckage to take place. A fire truck stood by, its hoses ready to put out any little flare-up that might suddenly show. People watched, and talked, and guessed, and expressed their outrage. The attack on Seth Harder and his farm was probably the result of a quarrel between the old man and his daughter's boyfriend, but the attack on the Town Hall was aimed at the whole community.

Uncle George was about to head across the street, where he saw Red Egan talking with Tom Andrews, publisher and editor of the *Journal*, Lakeview's weekly newspaper, when someone tugged at his sleeve. It was Joey, and standing just behind him was Ruby Harder, whose father had been burned to death just a few hours ago. Uncle George had seen Seth Harder's body roasting like a pig on a spit when he'd pulled Joey out of the burning barn at the height of the disaster. A normally pretty girl, dark hair, bright blue eyes, a disarming smile, she looked at this moment as though she'd been put through a wringer.

"Could you talk with Miss Ruby?" Joey asked.

"Of course I'll talk with her. I'm so very sorry for what's happened, Ruby," Uncle George said.

"They look at me as if I was some kind of a freak," Ruby Harder said in an unsteady voice.

"'They?' Who are 'they'?" Uncle George asked.

"Anyone I ask for help."

"My dear girl, I find that pretty hard to believe. Your father was liked, respected. People in town would do almost anything his daughter asked for—including me, Ruby."

"Not when I ask you for what I need," the girl said.

"Try me."

15

Ruby's lips drew together in a tight, thin line. "Help for Fletch Johnson," she said.

Uncle George felt a sensation of shock in the pit of his stomach.

"I've been to Mr. Graves," Ruby said. Foster Graves is Lakeview's one recognized attorney. "He says he can't help. He's my father's lawyer. He says he'll be handling my father's estate. He says—" Ruby's courage broke down.

"He says he can't defend his old friend's murderer," Joey said. "But every man is entitled to a fair trial, isn't he, Uncle George?"

"There is young Mr. Clifton who's just started a practice in town," Uncle George said.

"He told Miss Ruby that defending Fletch Johnson would make it certain he never made it here in Lakeview," Joey said.

Uncle George gestured across the street. "The fire's not really out yet," he said. "People will make a little more sense when they get over the shock of it all."

"But you don't need time, do you, Uncle George?" Joey asked.

"We need a place a little more private than this to talk," Uncle George said. "People are starting to move your way, Ruby. Everyone in town is going to want to ask you questions. Let's go around back of your house, Joey."

He didn't need time, but Uncle George knew he was going to have to make an honest decision for these two young people. If the fire at the Harder farm had been the only one that night, it would be easy to go along with the popular notion that Fletcher Johnson had gone off on a revenge kick. But add fire bombs and the destruction of the Town Hall to that and you have to wonder if there was any connection at all between the two disasters.

Uncle George and Joey and Miss Ruby headed for Esther's flower garden back of the drugstore. Miss Ruby was what the fifth-grade kids had called her before her tragedy. The local town school board had no choice but to dismiss her when she turned out to be pregnant. Her man had never reached the wedding ceremony. That meant a kind of fooling around that could only be a bad example for the kids.

Uncle George had often wondered how many of the young parents in town who had clamored for Ruby Harder's scalp when the unhappy situation was revealed had the right to "cast the first stone." Damn few, he thought.

Uncle George and Ruby sat on a white bench in Esther's garden, and Joey on the grass at their feet.

"Fletch needs legal help," Ruby said. "The two lawyers in town have both turned me down. Joey says you are probably the best lawyer in the world. I hoped you might at least advise us."

"Us?"

"Fletch and me," Ruby said. "I am going to marry Fletch, Mr. Crowder."

She didn't have very much luck with bridegrooms, Uncle George thought. "Even if he killed your father?"

"That's absurd, of course," Ruby said. "My father and Fletch quarreled. A lot of hot words and threats were spoken, but Fletch never in the world set fire to the farm."

"You believe that because you love him?" Uncle George asked.

"I believe that because I know him," Ruby said.

"Well, I'm not the best lawyer in the world, as the record will show, Ruby."

"But you're still licensed to practice law if you want to, aren't you, Uncle George?" Joey asked.

No one in the whole area had ever blamed George Crowder for the miscarriage of justice in which he'd been involved. As public prosecutor he'd taken a case worked up by the State Police, prosecuted the accused on the evi-

17

dence provided by the police, gotten a conviction. The police were responsible for a grim mistake, not the prosecutor. George Crowder's license to practice law had never been revoked or even suspended. It was his choice that he no longer practiced his profession. Back in those days when he'd been a successful lawyer and the County Attorney, Uncle George had depended on what he had later called "voodoo." He'd had a "gut feeling" about clients he chose to represent or alleged criminals he was authorized to prosecute. That gut feeling determined his course of action, and it had eventually failed him. He'd had a gut feeling about the man he'd sent to the gas chamber, a gut feeling that the man was guilty all the way down the line. His gut feeling had betrayed him. Too late, the man's innocence had been established beyond dispute. Unable to depend any longer on his inner convictions about a case, Uncle George had been forced to turn to something else to occupy his life.

"I can advise," Uncle George said, "but I can't act for you or Fletcher in any legal proceeding. That's long in the past for me. Has Fletch been arrested?"

Ruby nodded. "Held without bail. Charged with arson and second-degree murder. My father's. He's being held at the State Police barracks, but they plan to move him later this morning to the county jail."

"You've seen him, talked to him since the fire?"

"No. They'll only let family and his lawyer see him. He has no family. He doesn't have a lawyer. They say the court will appoint him an attorney, but that's not the same as having your own man."

"If you haven't seen him, how do you know—?"

The girl made an impatient gesture. "If someone told you that Joey had cut his mother's throat with a kitchen knife, would you believe it?"

"Of course not."

18

"Because you know him! Well, I know Fletch!"

"I guess you have a point there," Uncle George said. "You love someone, you know them. But—"

"You're saying that knowing Joey for all of his life and knowing Fletch for less than a year are two different things."

"Something like that."

"But you've always known what love was, haven't you, Mr. Crowder? Your parents, your sister, Joey, probably some woman I don't know about—"

Uncle George's face went unusually grim. If there had been a woman in his life, it was not public knowledge.

"I'd never known what it was to be loved until I met Brad Smith," Ruby said. "I don't have to write out that story for you, Mr. Crowder. The whole world knows it. I let myself be loved too soon." Her voice trembled. "I was so hungry for it."

"You had your father."

"My father never loved me," Ruby said. "My mother, whom I never knew, died giving birth to me. She was my father's whole life and he blamed me and hated me for what happened to her. He treated me reasonably well, fairly, because the whole town was watching to see how he would handle the situation. But there was never a loving touch or a loving word in private. Would you believe that when Brad was killed he said, 'I thought that, at last, I was going to get you out of my sight.'"

What a bastard, Uncle George thought.

"Then when it became apparent that I was going to have a baby, my father stopped pretending, even in public, that I was anything but a cross he had to bear. My boy was named after my father's father, not his own father as I wanted. He made himself Rod's legal guardian and held that as a club over me to blackmail me into being his slave."

"And then Fletcher Johnson?" Uncle George asked.

19

Ruby nodded, her eyes turned away. "Not what you're thinking, though, Mr. Crowder. Fletch and I never—never got close in a physical sense. But what my father saw, and what Davey Williams told the whole town, wasn't a cheap little necking spree. Fletch had asked me to marry him, and I'd said yes, and we were embracing."

"Your father wouldn't have let you marry."

"I'm of age, Mr. Crowder. He couldn't have stopped me except by using my child to blackmail me. Fletch convinced me that as my husband, he'd become Rod's legal guardian and my father couldn't do anything about it. That's true, isn't it, Mr. Crowder?"

"I think the courts would view it that way," Uncle George said.

"So will you help him, Mr. Crowder?"

Uncle George stared steadily at the girl for a moment. "Yes, I'll help him, Ruby."

"Bless you!" She reached out to clutch at his hands.

"Thanks, Uncle George," Joey said. "I knew you would."

"One or two questions, Ruby," Uncle George said. "The fire at your father's farm. Tell me how it started, what you know about that."

Ruby drew a deep breath. "We'd all gone to bed, my father in his room, Rod in his crib in my room with me. I was lying awake, not sleeping well. I heard this sound like an explosion, some kind of big truck or car backfiring. Then there was the flicker of flames against the wall of my room. I jumped out of bed and saw the barn, just back of the house, like a great torch burning in the night. It was then that I grabbed little Rod out of his crib and ran toward the door. Then I heard my father shouting 'Fire!'"

Uncle George glanced at Joey. "The fire bomb again. That ties the two fires together, don't you see? Same method, same arsonist." He turned back to Ruby. "Anyone else sleeping in the house or in the outbuildings?"

"Dave Williams has a room off the kitchen. I know I grabbed Rod up out of his crib and started downstairs. My father was in the front hall, calling the fire department on the phone. You didn't have to be an expert to see they would never get there in time. My father saw me and made a wild, sweeping gesture with his arms. 'Your lover's kept his word, you bitch!' he shouted at me. Then he ran out toward the barn. I could hear animals screaming, but I knew it was hopeless."

"You saw the house was going to go, too?"

"The kitchen wing had already caught," Ruby said. "I saw Dave Williams running after my father so I knew that, at least, all the people were safe. The heat from the flames was so intense I had to get little Rod as far away as possible. I was on a knoll back of the house when the fire department started to arrive. My father had gone into the barn. Dave Williams was out back, trying to drive some cows out of the corral there."

"You didn't see Fletch Johnson at any time while you were waiting for the fire company?"

"No! Because he wasn't there, of course."

"But he eventually came?"

"People seemed to come in waves," Ruby said. "First the fire truck with just a few men riding it. Then a wave of people in cars. Then a second wave. I think Fletch came with them. He spotted me out on the knoll with Rod and came running. He urged me to get farther away. 'This is going to be total, Ruby,' he said. I told him my father thought he, Fletch, had set the fire to get even. 'Anyone as sick as he is would think that way,' Fletch said. 'You know I didn't, don't you?' I told him I knew."

"You saw him again later?"

"No. Women came, among them Marilyn Stroud. She was the assistant principal at the school when I was a teacher there. She never turned her back on me. She insisted on driving me and Rod to her house in town. It was a couple of hours later that she brought me word that my father was dead and that Fletch had been arrested."

Marilyn Stroud, Uncle George knew, was a good lady, one of Esther's best friends. "Your boy is with Marilyn now?" he asked.

"I had to find you, Mr. Crowder," Ruby said, nodding an answer to his question. "She agreed with Joey that you were the person most likely to be helpful."

"So I'll do what I can, Ruby. Go to your boy and sit tight."

2

A small group of exhausted, angry men were gathered in Captain Purdy's office at the State Police barracks when Uncle George drove there in his jeep. Red Egan, the sheriff, was there along with Tom Andrews, the publisher of the *Lakeview Journal,* and a strange State Trooper who turned out to be Sergeant Terry, the arson expert from State Police Headquarters. Uncle George contributed what he had. Esther and Ruby, at two different fires, had heard explosions and Esther had seen a dark-haired boy she couldn't identify running from the Town Hall after the third explosion.

"That seems to link the two fires to the same person," he said. "Some kind of fire bomb in both cases. I don't quite know what I'm talking about when I say 'fire bombs.'"

"They're something a little bit new in our world," Terry, the arson expert, said. "Came in with the wave of terrorism around the world."

22

"What's terrorism got to do with Lakeview?" Captain Purdy asked. He was a big, blond, cold-eyed man.

"Nothing—necessarily," Terry said. "You ever stopped to figure how many billions of dollars are spent every year on illegal products like drugs, guns, other kinds of lethal weapons? Fire bombs are an elaboration of the wartime hand grenade. They are designed to start instant fires, break down impromptu defenses. They're a legitimate military weapon, illegal in the hands of a civilian. But they can be had by anyone if you know where to shop for them."

"But I take it you don't carry them around in your vest pocket," Uncle George said.

"Big as a hand grenade, and bigger," Terry said.

"So four of them have been set off in this town," Purdy said. "What does that tell us?"

Terry shrugged. "That they started four fires, three in one building complex."

"Would Fletcher Johnson have access to such bombs?" Purdy asked.

"He could," Terry said, "and so could you, or Mr. Andrews here, or Mr. Crowder, or Sheriff Egan."

"This man Johnson you have arrested apparently had a motive for harming Seth Harder for what happened a few weeks back, I understand. For a guess, something in Johnson's past made him aware of where he could get fire bombs. Took some time for him to get them, but when he had them, he struck."

"Why the Town Hall?" Uncle George asked.

"To create confusion. He succeeded in that, wouldn't you say, Mr. Crowder?"

"I'd like to talk to Fletch Johnson, Jim," Uncle George said to Captain Purdy.

"No way, George. Only family and his lawyer, if he gets one."

"He's got one. Me!"

23

Purdy brought his fist down on the desk. "If you're his lawyer, what the hell are you doing here?" he almost shouted.

"I'm your friend. I brought you valuable information. Now I tell you if Johnson wants me, I'll act for him."

Purdy, his pale eyes ice cold, turned to a trooper standing by the office door. "Take Mr. Crowder down to Johnson's cell." He turned back to Uncle George. "You play games with us, George, and so help me—"

Uncle George grinned at him. "People who make threats around here seem to get into big trouble, Jim."

The cell where Fletcher Johnson was being held was not for long-term imprisonment. It was neat, its interior painted white, with a wash basin and toilet, a cot, a single straight-backed chair. The trooper accompanying Uncle George announced to the prisoner that he had a visitor and unlocked the cell door to admit the caller.

"Mr. Crowder!" Fletch Johnson said.

He was a tall, dark, muscular, handsome young man. It wasn't a surprise that Ruby was attracted to him. Uncle George hadn't really known him, but he'd known who he was and had spoken to him casually as they passed in the village.

"Ruby asked me to come and see you," Uncle George said.

"How is she? Is she bearing up? The kid, Rod? How is he?"

"Both doing 'as well as can be expected'," Uncle George said. "There's a cliché answer to every question, I suppose. It's been a shocking experience for her, but mostly she's concerned about you. She says you haven't got a lawyer. I offered to represent you if you wanted me to."

"Want you? Having you as a lawyer puts me on the winning side in this town."

24

"You know why you've been arrested?"

"Sure. Dave Williams's story about my quarrel with old man Harder."

"He's dead, you know."

"Yeah. They told me here at the barracks. I didn't know that he was in the barn when I was there, but no one could have saved him."

"I know. I tried when I was rescuing Joey, my nephew, who was also trying. It was hopeless. He was pinned under a fallen beam. No way to pull him free and stay alive in the process."

"The cops think I set fire to the barn to get even for his trying to break up Ruby and me," Fletch said.

"Did you?"

"No way, and you wouldn't be here if you thought I had."

"I don't really know you at all, Fletcher—except that Ruby and my nephew, Joey, think you're top drawer. Tell me about yourself, where you came from, your family, your history."

The corners of Fletch's mouth drew down. "It's not all wine and roses," he said. "My father was a garage mechanic in Bennington, Vermont. My mother was a housekeeper for the college there. I went to school there, grew up there. I wasn't a bad kid, but I wasn't a good kid, I guess. Lot of hell-raising, but nothing real bad. After high school I was kind of at loose ends. I hadn't come up with any plans for the future, a career of any sort. There wasn't any money to send me to college. Then I ran into an older guy I'd always known. He'd gone into the army, got special training there, and eventually money for a college education when he'd served his enlistment time. So, I enlisted in the army."

"Special training?"

"Mechanics of one kind or another. I knew something for a starter, being around my old man all my life. Finally I was assigned to demolition. Explosives for blowing up bridges, buildings, fortifications. You know—if we were in real action."

Uncle George sat very still in the straight-backed armchair, staring at Fletch Johnson who was perched on the edge of the cot. "Teach you anything about fire bombs?" he asked.

"Run-of-the-mill stuff for setting buildings, fortifications, enemy encampments on fire."

"You know how to use them?"

"I must have set off dozens of them during our training," Fletch said.

Uncle George was silent for a moment. "Did you know that the fire at the Harder farm and the three fires that demolished the Town Hall were set off by fire bombs?"

Fletch just stared at Uncle George, and then a nerve twitched high up on his cheek. "Oh my God!" he said. "If you tell them what I've just told you, Mr. Crowder, they'll—they'll—"

"You just took me on as your lawyer, boy," Uncle George said. "What you've just told me is confidential, a matter between lawyer and client. But—"

"But what, Mr. Crowder?"

"How did you happen to wind up here in Lakeview, working as a farmhand for Seth Harder?"

"Farm work isn't what it used to be, horse and plow stuff," Fletch said. "It's all machinery these days: milking machines, tractors, trucks, mowers, water pumps—the works. A good-sized farm like Harder's, couple of hundred cows to be cared for and milked, needs to have a skilled mechanic as part of the work force. When I got out of the service, I took a job with a farm machinery agent in my hometown of Bennington. They got a call for help from Seth Harder. His milking machine was on the bum and he'd lost the man who'd been his machinery expert. My boss agreed to send someone and I was It."

26

"You came down here to fix Seth's milking machine?"

Fletch nodded. "Old machine. He was going to need a new one soon, but I could tell from the way he talked that he didn't want to have to get up that kind of money. I did what I could on the machine and agreed to wait around for the night milking to see if it worked properly. While I was standing around, watching the grass grow, I heard a sour sound coming from the engine of one of the farm trucks. I knew old man Harder had more trouble unless he had some work done on his transmission. I told him that and offered to have a look at it. He was grateful and his truck sounded like a Swiss watch ticking away when I got through with it. Harder, right then and there, asked me if I'd like to sign on permanently. Pay was about the same as I was getting. It would be something I could take a personal interest in. Just on impulse, I decided to do it." He smiled at Uncle George. "Believe it or not, I hadn't laid eyes on Ruby when I made up my mind."

"But you saw her later?"

Fletch nodded, and his face turned serious. "Every day, every meal in the farm kitchen where she worked like a slave. Ruby Harder—I thought she must be the old man's son's wife, but there was no son around. Then someone straightened me out. I heard the story of the bridegroom killed on the way to his wedding, and the later evidence that Ruby and her guy hadn't waited to get together until after a wedding that never happened." Fletch drew a deep breath. "We got to talking, mostly in the evenings after supper, sitting out back of the kitchen in the twilight. Daylight saving time. I found myself playing with little Rod and enjoying it. Piece by piece I was able to put together the story of Ruby's relationship with her father. Unreasonably, he hated her because her mother had died giving birth to her. That hatred was reinforced later when she subjected him to public shame by getting pregnant before

27

she was married. She wanted to escape and didn't know how with little Rod to take care of. All of a sudden I knew I was in love! I wanted her and the kid, wanted to take them away from Seth and out from under his cloud of hatred. That day—I was in the house to fix the washing machine—I got up the courage to ask her, and she said yes, and we were in each other's arms when the old man and Dave Williams barged in. You've heard the rest, I guess? Name callings, threats, and then he was aiming a gun at me and I was pretty damn sure he'd use it. So I left, telling him—and the whole world through Davey Williams—that I'd get back at him for this if it was the last thing I ever did."

"You left Seth's house but you didn't leave town, I know."

"I wasn't going without Ruby. But we had to plan it some way. How to get together for planning."

"And while you waited, you were planning a way to destroy Seth?"

"Taking Ruby and little Rod away from Seth wouldn't have destroyed him, it would have relieved him."

"You have some souvenirs of your military service, some fire bombs. You set one off in the Harder barns, and then, to keep the firemen from concentrating on putting out that fire, you set three more in the Town Hall complex, using some more of your souvenirs."

Fletch stood up from the cot, his jaw muscles rippling. "If that's the way you think it was, Mr. Crowder, there isn't much use in our talking any more."

"I didn't say that's the way I thought it was," Uncle George said, "but that's the way a lot of people are going to think it was. You don't have any kind of military souvenirs the cops can find, weapons of any sort?"

"No."

"If you wanted to get hold of some fire bombs, how would you go about it, Fletch?"

28

"What would I want them for?"

"Fourth of July, decided to use them for something else."

"That didn't happen, Mr. Crowder."

"But if you wanted to get some fire bombs, how would you go about it?"

Fletch hesitated. "Steal them," he said. "From any military base. Hundreds of them across the country. Perhaps some National Guard units are trained to use them."

"Nowhere else?"

"It's like everyone says . . . they are a weapon for terrorists. People always get rich off violence. Selling illegal arms tops the list."

"There aren't any military bases close by," Uncle George said.

"Relatively speaking—if you're talking about walking there!" Fletch said. "But New York isn't so far away by car, or Boston, or Albany."

"But it would be easier to buy those fire bombs from a crook than steal them from the army, wouldn't it?"

"Sure."

"How would you go about locating an illegal supplier?"

Fletch laughed. "Just stand around on a street corner in New York and wait for someone to ask you what you're waiting for. Someone will ask. There's always someone waiting to sell you drugs, or women, or weapons."

Uncle George stood up and held out his hand. "Ruby and my nephew Joey want me to take your case, son. But you're the one who has to hire me."

"I can't pay you," Fletch said.

"Getting the bastard who set these fires is all the pay I ask for, Fletch. Deal?"

The younger man gripped his hand. "Deal—gratefully accepted, Mr. Crowder."

*   *   *

29

Captain Purdy and Sergeant Terry, the arson expert, had left the captain's office when Uncle George returned there, but Tom Andrews, the *Journal*'s editor, was still there.

"Thought I'd wait to see what you decided about Johnson, George," he said.

"I've taken him on as a client," Uncle George said.

"That's news. I hope you're not putting your faith in a bad apple."

"My nephew, Joey, pointed out to me that every man is entitled to a fair trial, guilty or innocent. The rest of the legal talent in town doesn't seem to see it that way. So, I'm elected, I guess."

"Johnson is a lucky man," Andrews said. "You believe in him?"

"I believe Purdy and Terry have got to prove he's guilty."

"If I had what looked like a lost cause, I'd want you on my side, George," Andrews said. "By the way, a friend of yours was just here looking for you. Rich Nolan."

"I had a feeling he might be turning up," Uncle George said.

Richard Nolan had been one of Lakeview's big excitements some years ago, and Uncle George had played a role in his story. It had happened the year before the legal disaster that had ended George Crowder's career. Patrick Nolan had turned the town of Lakeview upside down twenty-five years ago. A wild-eyed, big, laughing, fun-loving Irishman had appeared out of nowhere and bought the Tolliver estate out on the lake. It didn't take long for the town to learn that their new citizen, a bachelor, was fabulously rich—oil, airlines, God knows what else. But Pat Nolan wasn't a rich man who spent what he had on luxuries for himself. He donated substantial sums to the local hospital, to the town library, to special improvements the community wanted. The town's fairy godfather, somebody called him. And in return? He just wanted friendship. The doors to his house on the lake were open to anyone, anytime of day or night. There was a playground for kids, ponies to ride, even a special lifeguard to watch over kids who swam off Pat Nolan's dock and the floats anchored offshore.

It was a day in spring that George Crowder got a call from Pat Nolan's houseman saying that Nolan wanted Crowder to come out to the house. An emergency, he was told.

At the house Uncle George found Pat Nolan stretched out in bed, looking pale, haggard.

"I appreciate your coming so promptly, Mr. Crowder," old Pat said. He patted at his chest with gnarled fingers. "Lung cancer. They give me a few weeks, couple of months at most."

"I'm sorry to hear that, Mr. Nolan."

"Not half as sorry as I am. I need someone to confide in, someone to help. I've chosen you out of all the people I know."

"If I can help some way, you know I'll be glad to."

"What I have to confide, George, is that I have a son."

"I didn't know you'd been married."

"I haven't," Pat Nolan said. "Long ago, many years before I came to America, I was in love with a girl in Ireland. It was before the big troubles of Irishmen against Irishmen, Irishmen against Englishmen, but there was too much anger and bad feeling for me to want to stay there."

"You had a son, you said."

The old man nodded. "I didn't know it till after I'd left Ireland for America. The woman who bore my child didn't have any use for me, and in those early days, I had myself to look out for. And then—well, I struck it rich, as you know. I could suddenly buy anything in the world I wanted. I could tell politicians how to vote! I was a powerhouse,

31

George, but I couldn't find my son. Living under some other name, probably his mother's, which was Flynn. I had private detectives looking for him. No luck."

"What can I do that you haven't already done?" George Crowder asked.

"I'm going to die—in a very short time," Pat Nolan said. "I want to draw up a will leaving literally hundreds of millions of dollars to a son I've never seen."

"That's pretty quixotic, isn't it?"

"That's the way I want it. I want him to have all the money, this property, everything I've got. You'll have to draw the will and then find him."

"All you'll have to do, I think, is print the story in the newspapers," Uncle George said. "He'll come forward."

And so the will was drawn, and the story, a fascinating one, was published and broadcast all around the world, particularly in Ireland. It was much talked about, much discussed, but in the few weeks that Pat Nolan lived on, there wasn't a ripple of a response from the heir to millions.

Pat Nolan died. George Crowder met with his disaster in the courts and left town. Months later a young woman appeared in town. Her passport and papers identified her as Mrs. Richard Nolan, wife of the missing heir. She'd come to America to find out if all the talk of millions was a hoax. Her husband was in the midst of the Irish violence and they'd imagined this was some kind of trick to get him away from the scene of action. Of course, if it wasn't, then he would come to claim his inheritance. The money would be happily used in his Irish cause.

It wasn't a hoax and Richard Nolan and his wife came to Lakeview to collect. As it turned out, they never left. They took over the big house on the lake and had been there ever since. Rich Nolan, a pleasant, quiet young man, was a far different personality than his flamboyant father. But his

32

generosity to community causes was equal to his father's. Mildred Nolan, his wife, busied herself with the hospital auxiliary and other local causes. They became popular members of the community, their generosity much appreciated.

Rich Nolan was chatting with someone in the parking lot when Uncle George came out of Purdy's office. Nolan had obviously been waiting for the older man because he broke off from his companion and came forward, smiling. Rich had inherited that smile from his father, and a shock of flaming red hair. His face, as Hector Trimble had once remarked, was "as Irish as Paddy's pig." He was tall, broad-shouldered, impressive in a way. He was, however, gentle and far from aggressive in his approach, completely opposite of his old man.

"Bad day for the home team," Nolan said, as he joined Uncle George. "I understand you're defending Fletcher Johnson."

"Advising him, at least," Uncle George said.

"You brought me very good luck once," Nolan said. "Maybe you will do the same for him."

"All your good luck came from a father with a conscience," Uncle George said. "Fletch's bad luck comes from people chewing on gossip."

"I can understand why he might have been angry and crazy enough to attack Seth Harder—even if it endangered Ruby and her youngster. But why the Town Hall?"

"And with fire bombs," Uncle George said.

"Fire bombs?" Rich showed his surprise.

"So far it's just a likely guess," Uncle George said. "People heard explosions at both places. They have to wait a little for the ashes to cool before they can rake them over for positive proof."

Rich shook his head. "In the country where I grew up

33

fire bombs are as regular as breakfast coffee," he said. "The whole Irish countryside lives on fire. That's what I wanted to talk to you about—the Town Hall fire."

"Oh?"

"I want the town fathers to know that I'll pay for the cost of rebuilding it. There's no way to replace the records or the historical mementos, but the building—I'd like to duplicate that for them. It was such a landmark. The big H."

"You thought about it, Rich? Probably run you into a million bucks."

"I can afford it."

"You didn't ask for advice, but I'll give it to you anyway," Uncle George said. "People are all too ready to accept a free ride. You offer to rebuild the Town Hall and they'll accept, sit back on their behinds, and do nothing—except for a couple of historical buffs who'll want it rebuilt 'just so.' If I were in your shoes, I'd make a different kind of offer. I'd offer to double anything the town raises for itself. There's insurance, of course, that won't half cover it. You would be the main contributor, but not the only one."

"I like it," Rich said. "You'll help me with it?"

"You won't need help. Let the town fathers know, and have your accountant ready to check their figures."

"One other thing, Mr. Crowder. Ruby Harder and her boy must be in pretty rough shape. I understand Seth Harder was up to his ears in debt."

"That's the talk."

"If Mildred and I could help, we'd like to. There's a guest cottage at our place she could use. A little eating money could be made available."

"You're a nice guy, Rich. I don't know what Ruby's story is, but I'll be talking to her in a bit. Shall I tell her what you've offered?"

"Please do," Rich said.

It had been a rough night and morning. Uncle George

34

headed his Jeep for Lakeview Mountain and his cabin where he knew Timmy, his setter dog, would be waiting anxiously. Uncle George needed a shower and a change of clothes before he headed for Marilyn Stroud's house in town where he guessed Ruby would be waiting with her young son. He could report to her then about his agreement with Fletch Johnson and Rich Nolan's offer of his guest cottage and a little food money on the side.

Timmy was ecstatic. Uncle George seldom went anywhere without him and the big red dog had spent anxious hours waiting. Uncle George stripped, shaved, and was in the shower when he heard Timmy announcing an approach. Timmy had different barks and this one welcomed a friend.

When he came out of the shower and put on fresh clothes, he found Red Egan waiting for him in the living room-kitchen of the cabin. He was playing with a police badge, which he dropped on the kitchen table when Uncle George appeared.

"Need you to sign on, George," Red said.

"What's up?" Uncle George had been willing to be deputized in the past.

"It's getting a little grim," Red said. "They've found a body in the south section of the Town Hall. It's totally burned, unidentifiable. A man is about all they know so far. Doc Walters is trying to find some way to put a name on him."

"Burns are that bad?"

"Charred bones is about it," Red Egan said. "Doc says there may be some kind of a dental pattern, but you have to have something to compare it with."

"Somebody local, trying to put out the fire, got trapped there?"

"Could be," Red said. "Almost has to be. Town Hall is closed up about six o'clock at night, except on special

35

occasions. Last night wasn't special. No one can get in after closing without a key. A couple of maintenance men, the town clerk himself, and a couple of office workers, both women, each have one. All those people are accounted for and so are their keys."

"So how did this burned-up character get in?"

"Two possibilities," Red said. "He saw the fire in the north and center sections, smashed a window, got into the south section hoping to prevent damage there. No way to prove that one way or another. Window frames all burned, gone."

"And the second guess?"

"Guy was in the building when it closed up for business at six o'clock. Wanted to stay there to steal something, find something. Or just some old creep who fell asleep in a corner somewhere and wasn't noticed when people closed up for the day."

"A fireman, one of the first to get there?"

"Damn near everyone from Lakeview was out at the Harder farm," Red said. "First fire company to get to the Town Hall was from Cornwell. They say there was no way anyone would try to get into the building, burning full blast. All their guys are accounted for."

"And you want me to—?" Uncle George started to ask.

"We've got to cover every family in this town, neighboring towns, find a report that someone's missing, not where they're supposed to be. Everybody knows you, George. They'll talk to you when they might freeze up before a State Trooper with that 'show me your license' kind of approach."

"This guy that was burned—could have been a tramp, just passing through town. People on the move all the time these days, Red. He sees a public building, a place where he'll find a bathroom, or a glass of water, or a place to sit down and rest his feet. Like you suggested, he could have

36

fallen asleep in a corner and wasn't noticed when people closed up for the day."

"It's worth a try," Red said. "We got a lot of ground to cover, George, unless we get lucky fast."

3

The problem that early afternoon was not to get people to talk, but to get them to stop talking so you could move on to the next family. Violent death had struck twice in the last hours, first Seth Harder at his farm, and then the stranger in the south wing of the Town Hall. But there was more to keep people jabbering. Somewhere there was someone armed with highly efficient fire bombs who could be looking for another target for his deadly weapons. A hundred people had a hundred theories, and discussing them with a knowledgeable person like George Crowder was heaven. Most of them leaned toward Fletch Johnson in the Harder fire, but why the Town Hall? Had the dead man there been a target, or just an accidental victim?

Uncle George found a pat way to close down most of the speculations from the people he questioned. "If you think Fletch Johnson is the villain, you can stop worrying about the chance of your being the next victim. Fletch is being held without bail in the county jail."

But as the day wore on, nobody was reported missing. Those burned bones in the Town Hall's south wing had been a living man this time yesterday, but today no one appeared to be missing. Twilight was fading at the end of the first day after the fires and Uncle George was returning to Lakeview not a bit wiser than he had been when he'd set out on his job for Red Egan. Everybody had theories, nobody had facts. No one appeared to be concerned over an absent family member or friend. The results of their afternoon efforts left Uncle George, Red Egan, and the State Troopers concluding that the dead man in the Town Hall wasn't local. The word had spread by word of mouth and over the local radio news and not a single person had come forward to express any kind of anxiety about anyone dear.

The sheriff's office was not very official looking. It was in the back of a store where Red Egan sold sporting equipment. Back of the store was a room that housed a pool table, a recreational hangout for a lot of local men. Next to it was the sheriff's office. Stew Miller, who tended the store, also handled messages for Red Egan when he wasn't there.

Red was still out on the road somewhere when Uncle George checked in. Stew Miller, a chunky, dark man in his fifties with a friendly nicotine-stained smile, reported that there was no news from Red or any messages that suggested anyone else had anything to report.

"Seems like that guy in the Town Hall chose the wrong place to take a nap," Stew said.

The phone rang on the counter just beside Stew Miller, and he picked it up. "Red Egan's Place. . . . Oh, hi!" He winked at Uncle George. "Speak of the devil. Yes, Red. Piece of luck. He's standing right here next to me." Stew held out the phone to Uncle George, who took it.

"Hi, Red. George here. You got something?"

"Got your feet braced?" the sheriff asked.

"For what?"

"Looks like your client has curved us all, George. Cops found two fire bombs of the type they think were used at Harder's and at the Town Hall left in Fletch's truck. They're bringing Fletch up from the county jail and it looks like they're ready to throw the book at him."

"State Police barracks?"

38

"Right. Purdy's office."

"Ten minutes," Uncle George said.

Nothing pleases a policeman more than solving a nasty crime in a hurry. Captain Purdy had to be proud of the way his men had reacted to Lakeview's night of death by fire. They had picked up Fletch Johnson at the Harder farm while they were still fighting the fire there. Suspicion of arson was the charge. They had searched Fletch's room at Mrs. Cain's boardinghouse in town and found nothing that would buttress their case. But later in the day, when most people were trying to find a "missing person" who could have been the burned man in the Town Hall, Trooper Thompson had gone back out to the Harder farm for a routine check, now that the burned buildings had cooled off enough for a search—evidence that would support the fire bomb theory.

Chatting with Dave Williams, the farmhand who'd been with Seth Harder when they walked in on Fletch Johnson and Ruby in a passionate embrace, Thompson got a report on the total disaster the blaze had been. Over two hundred cows had burned, expensive farm machinery, tools, the house and all its furnishings.

"Total wipeout," Williams was saying.

"Looks like there's one pickup truck left," Thompson said, pointing to a vintage Chevrolet parked about a hundred yards away from where the barn had been.

"Oh, that isn't Seth's truck," Williams said. "That belongs to Fletch Johnson. He must have drove it out here when the fire started."

"Or before he set it," Thompson said.

"I suppose. Cops arrested him, took him off, left the truck here. Probably didn't know it was his, or didn't bother to ask him how he got out here."

Thompson wandered down to the truck. Just routine—just so he could report on it to Captain Purdy. There was

39

nothing sensational about the truck—early 1970s, Thompson guessed. On the space back of the driver's seat and the rear window of the cab was a large brown paper bag. Idly, Thompson opened the bag to look inside and froze after one brief, profane shout.

Out of the bag he produced a sort of carton, like the ones eggs come in from the supermarket. This carton was made for six giant-sized eggs. There were two of them still in place.

"Look like hand grenades," Dave Williams said.

"Or fire bombs," Thompson said.

A small squad of specialists were gathered in Captain Purdy's office when Thompson turned up with his find. There was Purdy himself, Ben Bowers, the fire chief, Carl Carpenter, the newly appointed County Attorney, and Sergeant Bill Terry. They were listening to Red Egan's account Thompson arrived. There was no question about what he'd found in that brown paper bag in Fletch Johnson's truck.

"They're fire bombs," Sergeant Terry said. "Well-known brand, manufactured by a company named Hitchcock somewhere in Pennsylvania. Used by the military here and all over the globe. Suspected of being sold illegally to terrorist groups—here, the Middle East, Africa, South America, the Philippines, what have you."

"How would Johnson get hold of them?" Carpenter, the County Attorney, asked.

Terry shrugged. "His history—shouldn't be too difficult. Old army contacts still with access to supplies, black-market operators you can always find if you know what you want to buy."

"The bombs always come in that kind of carton—like eggs?" Purdy asked.

"Standard small-size packaging," Terry said. "Of course,

if you're supplying an army group they're crated or cartoned."

"No use guessing where Fletch got them," Purdy said. "Let's get him up here and ask him."

"Your Mr. Johnson seems to have just about signed his own death sentence," Terry said. "Two counts of murder, at least second-degree murder, two counts of arson. There were six bombs in that carton. He used one at the Harder farm and three at the Town Hall. I wonder what his plans were for the other two?"

Uncle George arrived at Purdy's office before Fletch Johnson was brought in from the county jail. Technically, the police didn't have to share their information with him, but it didn't occur to Captain Purdy and the others to block him out. He was too well known, too much respected.

"How well do you know your client, Mr. Crowder?" Carl Carpenter, the County Attorney asked.

"Not well," Uncle George said.

"What persuaded you to take him on as a client? I understood you'd given up any active practice."

"George has a right to practice if he wants," Red Egan said. "He's still got an active, working license."

"I'm not questioning that," Carpenter said. "But why take on a stranger when the presumption of guilt is so obvious?"

"I, of course, didn't know about these fire bombs you've found in his truck," Uncle George said. "A person I care for and trust asked me to help Fletch."

"You mind telling me who?" Carpenter asked.

Uncle George hesitated. "My nephew, Joey Trimble."

"A teenaged boy?"

"I trust Joey's instincts about people better than most," Uncle George said. "Ruby Harder also asked for my help."

"The girl all the trouble between Harder and Johnson was about?"

"I also talked with Fletch here in jail. I decided to help him as best I could."

Carpenter's smile was twisted. "You think maybe ten years absence from the practice of law has made you a little oversentimental, Mr. Crowder?"

"Perhaps—if Fletch can't explain those fire bombs," Uncle George said.

"He's about to have his chance," Captain Purdy said. Standing by the office window, he'd seen the police car arrive, bringing Fletch Johnson from the county jail.

A day behind bars hadn't improved Fletch Johnson's appearance. He hadn't shaved for one thing, and a thin stubble of dark beard shadowed his face. His eyes looked swollen with fatigue. He looked tense and nervous until he saw Uncle George, and then he managed a smile.

"Feel a little better seeing you here, Mr. Crowder."

"You have rights, Fletch," Uncle George said. "You don't have to answer questions if you don't want to. Whatever you do say, they can use against you."

"I've got nothing to hide, Mr. Crowder."

The County Attorney seemed to be in charge. He stepped forward, holding one of the fire bombs in the palm of his hand. "You know what this is, Johnson?"

Fletch leaned closer. "Sure. It's a fire bomb, a Hitchcock. I handled dozens of them in the army."

"And one at Harder's and three at the Town Hall last night," Carpenter said.

"You're kidding," Fletch said.

"You know, of course, where we found this and another one," Carpenter said, pointing to the second bomb in the carton on Purdy's desk.

"How would I know that?"

42

"They found the two bombs in that carton, in a brown paper bag, in your truck at the Harder farm," Uncle George said.

Fletch's swollen eyes blinked. "Now you really are kidding!"

"Trooper Thompson found them in the presence of a witness, Dave Williams," Uncle George said.

"So let's stop playing games," Purdy said. "I think we'll be able to prove that the four bombs missing from that carton were used to set the two fires. That just about cooks your goose, Johnson."

Fletch reached up and pressed the tips of his fingers against either side of his forehead. Then he looked at Uncle George. "Just for the record, Mr. Crowder, I never saw those bombs before, never owned any, never used any, certainly never stashed any in my truck."

"I wouldn't expect you to say anything else at this point," Carpenter said. "I expect you'll have some fancy explanation as to how they got in your truck."

Fletch shook his head, slowly. "I can't even make a guess," he said.

"You mind, Carpenter, if I ask Fletch a couple of questions, in your presence, ones I'll ask him anyway in private?" Uncle George put in.

Carpenter made a tired gesture of consent. Everyone was tired.

"Tell us, Fletch, about coming to the Harders' to fight the fire."

Fletch drew a deep breath. "I was asleep in my room at Mrs. Cain's when the siren sounded," he said. "Mrs. Cain was already at the phone when I got there, told me it was the Harder farm."

"And you went to help your enemy?" Carpenter asked.

"I went to help the woman I love and her kid," Fletch

43

said. "I started toward the Harders' in my pickup, saw Joe Stearns, who lives next to Mrs. Cain, headed there on foot. I stopped, picked him up, drove him out there with me."

"He might have noticed whether there was a brown paper bag on the shelf of the seat in your truck," Uncle George said.

"He might or he might not," Carpenter said. "His mind was on a fire, not what was in Johnson's truck."

"So you got to the Harders'," Uncle George said.

"Even at a distance we saw it was gone," Fletch said. "I parked about a hundred yards from the barn. Stearns went his way, and I went looking for Ruby and Rod."

"You found them?"

"Yes, watching from a knoll some distance away. Ruby told me her old man was in the barn, God help him."

"Did you offer to help him?" Carpenter asked.

"There were dozens of professional firemen down there," Fletch said. "I just wanted to get Ruby and Rod somewhere safer. Before I could get very far with that a couple of troopers arrested me."

"Pretty quick on the trigger, weren't they?" Uncle George asked Captain Purdy.

"Not under the circumstances," Purdy said. "A couple of weeks ago Seth Harder came to us and told us he'd been threatened by Johnson. My men knew that. When they saw Johnson out there, it was logical to pick him up for questioning."

"So there were no bombs in your truck, Fletch?" Uncle George asked.

"You say they were found there," Fletch said, "but I didn't put them there. I never saw them, never owned them, nor any others. Never handled one since I got out of the army."

"You have an enemy who would want to frame you?" Uncle George asked.

44

"The only enemy I had in the whole damn world was Seth Harder," Fletch said. "Ask around. I have no other enemies that I know of."

"Somebody knew how damning it would be for those fire bombs to be found in that truck," Uncle George said. "Someone who knew about your army history, someone who knew about your quarrel with Seth."

"And someone who had a carton of fire bombs," Carpenter said. "Come on, Crowder, that frame-up idea just won't stick. Haven't we had enough of this, Purdy? By the time Crowder gets through with this, he'll have a whole fairy story invented . . ."

Purdy nodded. "I guess that's about all the time there is for this, George."

"Next stop, the grand jury," Carpenter said.

Uncle George's face looked carved out of rock. "Don't start celebrating too soon, Carpenter," he said. "There are too many unanswered questions for you to let yourself think you're on easy street."

"What questions?"

"The dead man in the Town Hall. Who was he and how did he die?"

"A tramp who took shelter there, fell asleep, and died of toxic smoke inhalation and by fire."

"Or was murdered, his body hidden in the Town Hall, and the fire set to hide the evidence of a crime."

"Here we go again," Carpenter said. He gave Fletch Johnson a twisted smile. "You murder some guy, hide the body in the Town Hall, set fire to it, and then torch the Harder farm so everyone would think that that was the target?"

"You've got it in the wrong order, Carpenter," Uncle George said. "The fire at the Harder place first, set off by a fire bomb, according to Miss Ruby. The siren sounded, everybody headed for there. Fletch was one of them, with

Stearns, to whom he gave a lift, a witness. He didn't leave Harder's and the cops arrested him there. The fire in the Town Hall came when he had an alibi, easily verified by Stearns, Ruby Harder, little Rod, and Purdy's men. Fletch didn't throw three bombs into the Town Hall and all of you have to know it by now. My sister saw a young boy run away from the Town Hall seconds after the third bomb exploded. He may or may not have been responsible, but he was there. If one person is responsible for both fires, he can't be Fletcher Johnson, and your own people will have to testify to that. So does that sound like a fairy story, Carpenter?"

"I imagine Carpenter won't sleep as well as he thought he would," Red Egan said. He and Uncle George were standing together in the parking lot at the police barracks. They had just watched the County Attorney drive away, not looking cheerful. "You believe your own story, George? Or were you just defending a client?"

"I believe it," Uncle George said, "but there are gaps that need filling in."

"Such as?"

"How did the man in the Town Hall die? Was he just someone who fell asleep, unnoticed, and was burned in the fire, or was he murdered and the fire set to cover the crime? If it was just someone who fell asleep, it's hard to connect the two fires, set by one man with fire bombs. If it was murder, then the Harder fire was set so the whole town was looking the other way while the murdered man's body was stashed in the Town Hall and the place torched to hide any evidence of a crime."

"But it didn't quite work," Red Egan said. "They found the man's skeleton."

"But so far the killer is safe—until we can identify the body. If we could identify the dead man, that would supply us with a lead to his enemy."

"Somebody robbed, tossed into the Town Hall, no lead at all—if it was just a mugging? Fire started for some other reason altogether, started by someone armed with fire bombs ready to start a big blaze."

Uncle George rubbed the back of his hand against his chin. "And a question I need answered—for me and for Fletch Johnson. Could those fire bombs be set off by remote control? If so, Fletch's alibi is no alibi. He has the technical knowledge, if there is such knowledge. If those bombs could have been set in advance, exploded at a later time from some distance away, Fletch's alibi begins to unravel."

"There's a guy over there who probably has the answer," Red said. He pointed at Sergeant Terry, the state's arson expert, who was approaching his car. Red waved and they hurried toward him.

"Mr. Crowder has a question he needs answered," Red said to the trooper.

"That doesn't surprise me," Terry said. "According to my people, Mr. Crowder's invented something out of whole cloth. What's your question, Crowder?"

"Could those Hitchcock fire bombs be planted in the Town Hall, detonated later from some distance away—remote control?"

"No way that I know of," Terry said promptly. "The Hitchcocks are what we call a 'contact explosive.' They go off on contact. They're tricky to handle, which is why the army trains special men to use them. You pull the pin on them, like a hand grenade, and toss them. They go off on contact. Scared the hell out of me watching those guys in there tossing those two live ones around. Dislodge one of the pins and you could drop one on your foot and blow up the whole joint."

"So my client couldn't have fire bombed the Town Hall from the Harder farm?"

"Oh, there's a way," Terry said.

Uncle George braced himself for the answer.

"He could have an ally, an accomplice," Terry said. "Johnson sets up his alibi and his ally sets off the bombs at the Town Hall."

It was an answer—an answer without proof, but an answer.

"My sister saw a boy running from the Town Hall just after the third bomb exploded," Uncle George said. "Just his back, but a boy."

"I know," Terry said. He gave Uncle George a strange, tight-lipped look and turned to Red Egan. "You protect me, Sheriff, if I give your friend a guess he won't like?"

Red laughed. "I'll protect you, Sergeant."

"I understand, Mr. Crowder," Terry said, "that you were persuaded to take on Johnson as a client by your nephew, Joey Trimble."

"Joey steered me to him, I took him on at his own face value," Uncle George said.

"But Joey was his friend, right? A boy running from the Town Hall after the third bomb was fired—?"

Uncle George's jaw muscles rippled. He took a quick step forward, stopped—and laughed. "Esther wouldn't know her own son?"

"I'm sure she would," Terry said. "Back, front, upside down. But would she say so?"

"Why not describe a giant of a man who couldn't possibly be Joey?"

"Couldn't think fast enough under pressure."

"What pressure?"

"You, her husband, anxiety for her boy."

"She says the boy she saw had dark hair. Joey's a blond."

"So, she thought a little bit under pressure. So, calm down, Crowder. I don't have a shred of proof, but it's an

48

idea that may come up when they start thinking about an accomplice."

Uncle George was silent for a moment. "But no way for remote control?"

"Not unless some genius has come up with something I don't know about. A machine that will pull the pin, throw the bomb where you want it to go? I think not. So who were Johnson's pals aside from your nephew and his girlfriend?"

"Ruby has an alibi, too, you know," Uncle George said. "Hundreds of people saw her and young Rod after the fire started at Harder's and before the Town Hall went up."

"But she and your nephew might tell you who Fletch Johnson's ally might be," Terry said. "But, then, you're not likely to nail down the lid on your client's coffin, are you?"

The two friends watched Sergeant Terry drive off into what was now night.

"They're really set on Fletch Johnson, aren't they?" Red Egan said.

Uncle George watched the red taillights of Terry's car disappear. "If I were on the other team," he said, after a moment, "I'd be waiting for someone to prove me wrong. I'd be worried about the dead man in the Town Hall, but not too worried. Accident. I'd have the bombs that were used to start the fire in Fletch Johnson's truck. I'd have Fletch Johnson who has a motive for the Harder fire. I'd have Fletch Johnson who knows and was trained how to handle those bombs, had access to them, almost certainly, through past connections. How much more would I need?"

"But you're still hanging in there for Fletch?"

Uncle George nodded. "I hate to use the words, Red. They already wrecked me once. But I have a gut feeling—"

4

It had been a long and grueling day for Dr. Walters. He was not only almost everyone's personal physician in Lakeview, he was also the town's medical officer when the police needed his services. On this day he had been involved with two autopsies, one on Seth Harder and one on a collection of burned bones found in the Town Hall. In addition, dozens of people involved in fighting the fires had come to him with minor burns and cuts rather than go to the emergency room at the hospital, which was also over-run. He couldn't, however, turn away George Crowder, who was an old valued friend.

"Word's around that you're defending Fletch Johnson," the doctor said when he and Uncle George were settled in his office.

"That's the way it is, Bill."

"How can I help?" the doctor asked. "Understand, I mean help you, not Fletch Johnson."

"Like most of the people in town, you're convinced about him?"

"I'm never convinced by gossip, George, but I haven't heard anything that would make me lean another way," the doctor said. "So tell me."

"I've just finished telling Red that if I had my old job as County Attorney, I'd think I had a case," Uncle George said.

"But—"

"It's too pat. It's too good, Bill. And there are too many unanswered questions."

"And you think I may have answers?"

"You may have something that would point me toward answers."

"I'm not an expert on fire bombs," the doctor said.

"But you're an expert on dead people. The man in the Town Hall, Bill—?"

The doctor's face stiffened. "Charred bones," he said. "Enough for me to be certain it was a male, full grown. I'd guess middle-aged, in his forties—but that's only a guess. Nothing else, not even teeth that could be compared with a dental chart in some dentist's office. No clothing—no nothing. Let me give you one of my guesses."

"Please do."

"I think that guy—whoever he is or was—got the full impact of that bomb; that it landed right on him or right beside him. He didn't just burn up in the fire. He was destroyed by the explosion."

"Accident," Uncle George said.

"Maybe. But let me tell you that the body was lying right in the center of the reception room in the south wing."

"Proving what?"

"Suggesting that he wasn't overlooked by the people closing up at six o'clock," the doctor said.

"As devil's advocate, I'd have to say it doesn't prove that. The man was out of sight, overlooked by the people who closed up, later was wandering around when the bomb hit."

"And arguing for you, George, I'd say the body was placed there, dead or unconscious. The bomber had to get far enough away from the impact of the explosion to be safe himself. He leaves the body where he can see it from outside a window."

"How did he get the body into the south wing after the place was locked up for the night?" Uncle George asked.

"We don't know and we'll never know," the doctor said. "A door forced, a window smashed; fire destroyed any way of proving that."

"Give me one last guess," Uncle George said. "Why risk destroying all three wings of the building when he only needed to destroy that body in the south wing?"

"To confuse you," the doctor said, smiling. "He had the bombs. He wanted to obscure the real motive. He had Fletch Johnson already set up as a fall guy. He wants it to look like a crazy man at work. I'll bet you a good steak dinner, George, that when you find him, you'll also find that he had a hell of a lot driving him. This isn't just anger at Seth Harder for ordering a man out of his house. There is something much bigger than that on the line to justify a holocaust."

"So the unconscious or dead man is placed in the south wing," Uncle George said. "Then a bomb is thrown into the north wing, then a second bomb into the center section, and only then the bomb in the south wing to obliterate the dead man. Why risk those first two bombs?"

"Think it through, George. The first bomb was thrown at the Harder farm. The whole town starts heading north. The killer goes south, probably with his victim in the car he's driving. The coast is completely clear here in town for him to get the body into the south wing. Everyone has either gone to or is thinking of the Harder fire. The killer gets that body into the south wing. He has ammunition to spare— still five bombs out of a carton of six. He doesn't want to focus attention on the south wing, so he goes north, center, and south. Whole thing doesn't take more than two or three minutes. Now he goes back out to the Harder place, puts the two remaining bombs in that brown paper bag in Johnson's truck, and he's home free—except for one George Crowder."

"Ask you a question, Bill?" Uncle George asked. "Why do you practice medicine?"

"I don't get it. It's my thing—medicine."

"I ask because you're so good at my thing—crime," Uncle George said.

Nobody was "early to bed" in Lakeview that night. There was too much to talk about, and a large section of the male

52

population was out on the streets, patrolling. There could be a dangerous pyromaniac floating around somewhere. There's an ugly thing that happens at a time like that. A man can't be quite sure of his own brother.

Uncle George stopped his Jeep outside Marilyn Stroud's cottage, located on the other side of the shopping center's parking lot from the Trimbles' pharmacy and home. Esther and Marilyn Stroud had grown up together and were thick as thieves. Marilyn had never married and she treated Esther's Joey as though he were her own. She was "Aunt Marilyn" to Joey, even though she was the assistant principal of his school and considered a "tough customer" by other kids. Uncle George had hoped to find Ruby and her small son and Joey at Marilyn's, and he was right about them. He hadn't wanted to talk to Joey in front of Hector, the boy's father. Passing along Sergeant Terry's notion that Joey might have been Fletch Johnson's accomplice in last night's horror in front of Hector Trimble would have resulted in an explosion heard 'round the world.

Marilyn and her house guests were in the kitchen, enjoying a before-bed snack—some ham and cheese sandwiches on some of Marilyn's homemade bread, and one of her apple pies, which Uncle George remembered from long ago. Little Rod Harder was nodding in his chair. Ruby took him away. Uncle George meant "news" and Ruby didn't want her listening interrupted.

"Is there anything new, George?" Marilyn Stroud asked.

"You know about the fire bombs being found in Fletch's truck?"

"Clearest frame-up I ever heard of," Joey said.

"I hope," Uncle George said.

"You hope? You don't *know*?" Joey was outraged.

"Wait till you hear what they're playing with about the Town Hall fire. They think Fletch had an accomplice and that he just might be you—the boy your mother saw leaving after the third bomb went off in the south wing."

"Of course she wouldn't have recognized me," Joey said.

"She wouldn't have admitted it was you."

"Bunk!" Joey said. "If Mom thought I'd committed a crime, she wouldn't have covered for me."

"So maybe she didn't recognize you, just saw your back in retreat."

"With long, dark hair!" Joey said. "Come on, Uncle George."

"How idiotic can they get?" Ruby asked from the doorway.

"Part of a policeman's job when he doesn't have a vital piece of evidence," Uncle George said, "is to invent a piece that will fit with the ones he's got. Then he waits for someone to knock it down."

"And so they invent Joey?" Ruby's outrage was doing her good.

"But you are Fletch's friend, aren't you, Joey?" Uncle George asked.

"Of course!"

"As long as they're thinking 'accomplice,' all Fletch's friends will be suspect," Uncle George said. "Your Mom saw a 'boy' running from the south wing. Until the troopers can find another 'boy' who was Fletch's friend, you're going to rate high on the accomplice list, Joey."

"That's crazy! Why would I throw a fire bomb in the Town Hall?"

"Because Fletch, your friend, asked you to."

"I just say 'Yes, Fletch' and set fire to the Town Hall?"

"If I asked you to?" Uncle George asked.

Joey looked steadily at his beloved Uncle George. "If you asked me to, I'd know it was the right thing to do."

Uncle George reached out and put his hand on the boy's shoulder. "I promise I won't ever betray your confidence in me, boy."

"I know you'd never ask me to do anything wrong," Joey said. "Also if my Mom asked me. But no one else."

"And if it was a crime, and this was a crime—?"

"No way," Joey said.

Uncle George's arm slipped around the boy's shoulders and held firm for a moment. Then he turned to Ruby. "Who are Fletch's friends, Ruby?"

The girl's fighting spirit was up. "You expect me to help the troopers, Mr. Crowder?"

"I expect you to help me help Fletch's friends," Uncle George said. "If I don't know who they are, I can't be much use to them, can I?"

Ruby turned toward the window and stood looking out into the night. Marilyn Stroud touched Uncle George's arm. "Coffee?" she asked.

He nodded but didn't speak, waiting for Ruby. The girl finally turned back from the window.

"Please don't think I'm stalling, Mr. Crowder, when I tell you I don't know much about Fletch's friends—not friends who would go out on a limb for him. I've told you Fletch and I are going to be married, but I haven't known him so very long; only a couple of months. My father made it hard for us to spend time together, and when we did, we talked about ourselves and our future and not about other people."

"Two months isn't a long time, but you saw him every day, ate meals with him every day. A lot of that time was with your father present. Did you get meals for Dave Williams and other people who worked at the farm? You understand what I'm getting at, Ruby. There has to have been some talk about his life in general. 'I saw Joe Blow on the street today. Just bought a new car.' That would mean to me that Joe Blow was something more than a name on a mailbox to him."

Ruby hesitated. "I don't particularly remember things like that. The thing with us—Fletch and me—started only a few days after he came to work for my father. First it was as a repairman for a farm machinery company. Then my

55

father asked him to stay on permanently. How can I tell you? My father didn't notice that something was happening between Fletch and me almost the second day."

"Fast worker, Mr. Johnson," Uncle George said.

"Fletch didn't 'work' on me," Ruby said. "I—I didn't flirt with him. It was more like turning on a light switch. The light came on that first or second day and it burned bright and clear for both of us."

"Love at first sight," Uncle George said.

"I'd heard about it, but I didn't really believe it could happen until I met Fletch. When we had any privacy, I had so much I had to tell him. There was little Rod always there. I had to tell him about the man who died on the way to his wedding, about how I'd been a little too quick to let myself be loved. None of that mattered to Fletch. He didn't have anything that important to tell me. He'd grown up in Bennington, gone through high school there, and then the army. Moving from place to place there'd been girls, but no one important. He never talked about friends. I suppose you mean men friends when you ask, Mr. Crowder?"

"I suppose. Tossing fire bombs around isn't exactly a pastime for girls."

"There certainly wasn't anyone in the army so close to him he thought it was worth talking about," Ruby said. "Here? He worked on the farm all day, had supper in our kitchen, helped me clean up afterward and stayed to talk as long as my father would allow. He didn't circulate here in Lakeview. He knew Dave Williams, of course, and some of the store people, and I suppose people who sold mechanical equipment and supplies for the farm. But he didn't have friends, really." The girl's smile brightened her face. "The electric light switch had been turned on, and all we were interested in was each other. A friend who would bomb a building for him? That's absurd, of course."

"Did he ever mention what he did in the army?"

"Not much. More about the places he'd been. The Middle East, Lebanon, Egypt, eventually the invasion of Grenada."

"He mention that he was involved with explosives?"

"Isn't everybody in the army?" Ruby asked.

The quiet of the night was suddenly destroyed by the sound of the fire siren. Uncle George stood very still, listening. Marilyn Stroud went to the phone and asked the operator where the fire was. She turned away from the phone, her eyes wide and frightened.

"It's your cabin on the mountain, George!"

Part Two

1

When other people suffer a loss you can feel regret, sadness, even shock. When the harm is aimed at you, the wound is far deeper.

The cabin on the mountain was very precious to Uncle George. He had built most of it with his own hands, equipped it with special gadgets for his own pleasure, come to like the idiosyncrasies of the daily life that had been created by living there. Destruction by fire was unthinkable. It couldn't be the result of any carelessness. He'd given up smoking long ago. There hadn't been a fire in the fireplace for several days, no way there could have been a leftover coal or hot ash. An electrical short? He had his own generator powered by a gasoline engine located in a shed about twenty yards away from the cabin. He prayed that was where the trouble might be as he drove his Jeep toward the mountain, young Joey clinging to the passenger seat beside him.

When they hit the narrow dirt road leading up the mountain, they were slowed to a crawl. The fire engine and the cars of volunteers were crowded up ahead of them. Uncle George couldn't see any signs of flames against the night sky. Were they in time, or were they too late? Fire could have burned for a long time up here before anyone might spot it.

They broke into the clearing at the top of the road. A ring of car headlights was focused on the cabin which, at least on the outside, appeared to be intact.

"Looks okay," Joey said.

"Inside can be a shambles," Uncle George said.

Ben Bowers, the local fire chief, came around from the far side of the fire truck and headed toward the Jeep.

"You got lucky, George," he said. "Very little damage, thanks to Bob Reed."

Bob Reed was another local man who had grown up in Lakeview with Uncle George, an old friend. He had a small chicken farm just down at the foot of the hill and a little south of the cabin.

"Foxes been raiding his coops," Bowers went on. "He set some traps just up above you."

"I know," Uncle George said. "He warned me about them because of Timmy." Where was Timmy? The dog almost always came charging out to greet him. Too much excitement, Uncle George thought.

Bowers, a lanky, suntanned man with thinning brown hair, went on. "Like most of us, Bob's been involved most of the day at Harder's and then the Town Hall. He went up the hill after dark because he wanted to check his traps. Didn't like to think of animals trapped and hurting—even if they were foxes. He was just a few yards above your place, heading up, when he heard the sound of shattering glass, and then what he thought was a gunshot. He called out. When no one answered, he came all the way down to here. There was a light on in that back pantry of yours. He could see a little stream of smoke coming out of what looked like a broken window. It turned out to be the top half of the back door. Glass, right?"

Uncle George nodded.

"Then Bob saw the door was standing an inch or two open. He went in and saw a fire burning in a trash basket under the table there. Table was starting to burn, and the floorboards were smoking. You'd better hear the rest from him. He's talking to Captain Purdy over behind the fire truck."

Uncle George and Joey followed the fire chief over to where Captain Purdy was taking notes from a statement being made by Bob Reed, a stocky little gray-haired man, who was dragging on a cigarette as though his life depended on it.

"No rest for the weary," Purdy said.

Uncle George was focused on Bob Reed. "I owe you, Bob," he said.

"You'd do the same for me," Reed said. "I just got lucky, being here when it happened."

"That's what we're trying to figure out," Purdy said. "What happened?"

Reed repeated the part of the story Ben Bowers had already told Uncle George. "When I got inside and saw the fire, I grabbed that trash basket and threw it outside. I pumped some water into a pail you have there and poured it on the table and the floor that was starting to burn. Then I called the fire company. I couldn't be sure I would control it all by myself."

"You mentioned a gunshot," Uncle George said.

Reed shrugged. "I know a gunshot when I hear one," he said. "As soon as I had things under control, I went into the main part of the cabin, calling for you—or anyone. There was no one."

"Someone fired the glass out of the door so he could reach inside and open it," Uncle George suggested.

"No way," Reed said. "The breaking glass is what I heard first. The gunshot came later. After I called the fire company, I drew another pail of water, went outside, and doused that burning trash basket before it set fire to the woods."

"You didn't see anyone running away when you came?"

"No."

"How would the person know you were coming?"

"Well, I shouted when I heard the gunshot. Started running and shouting as I ran toward the cabin."

"If it weren't for the gunshot," Captain Purdy said, "we'd have to think the fire was an accident—something left smouldering in that trash basket that finally caught."

"And smashed the glass out of the door?" Uncle George asked.

"I guess not," Purdy said. "There was someone here who got away."

"All he had to do was go into the cabin and out the front door, the other side from where I was coming," Reed said.

"If a gun was fired there has to be a bullet somewhere," Uncle George said.

"Or in someone!" Purdy said.

"Let's have a look inside," Uncle George said.

"I've got a man taking prints of the door handle, inside and out," Purdy said. "Stay out of his way. Not much hope because Bob handled both sides before he thought about anything but putting out the fire."

The back "pantry" was really just a large room, lined with shelves and the door to one large closet. The table in the center of the room and the floor under it where the trash basket had stood showed how close things had been to a total fire. Only Bob Reed being yards away had saved the place.

Uncle George and Purdy began searching the walls for some place a bullet might have lodged. Over the sound of voices, inside and out, Uncle George heard a faint, whimpering wail. He stopped dead in his tracks. Timmy!

Uncle George hurried into the main section of the cabin, calling to his setter dog. The whimpering wail came again and Uncle George, down on his hands and knees, found the big red dog sprawled out under his master's bed.

"Timmy!" It was Joey this time, down on the floor beside his uncle.

Gently, they pulled the dog out from under the bed. The dog's right shoulder was bloody, his right front leg pulled

64

up under him, quivering when Uncle George touched it with gentle fingers.

"Been shot," Purdy said from behind them.

"This guy is my best friend," Uncle George said. "I've got to get him to the vet's."

"I want the bullet if it's there," Purdy said.

Later, it wasn't too difficult to put together what had happened. In the bottom of a side door to the cabin was a swinging panel. Timmy would push it from the inside to get out, and from the outside to get in. Timmy, left alone for a long time, had decided he wanted to be inside after dark. Had anyone come in a car he would have barked a warning whether there was anyone to warn or not. Bob Reed would have heard that if he hadn't heard the car. The intruder had broken the glass in the pantry door. Timmy, the defender, must have rushed there from wherever he was sleeping, barked and growled at the intruder, and grabbed at the hand that was reaching through the broken glass to unlock the door from the inside. The intruder had shot the dog. He'd gone in, started the fire—and heard Bob Reed calling. He'd had to escape before the job was thoroughly done. Timmy had crawled away to the safe cover of Uncle George's bed and stayed silent till he heard Uncle George's voice.

Uncle George and Joey lifted the wounded dog onto a blanket and between them carried him out to the Jeep. Captain Purdy was to notify Dr. Kellog, the veterinarian, that they were coming and to preserve the bullet if it was still lodged in the wounded animal. Underway, Uncle George reached a hand back and felt a slippery tongue lick his fingers.

"It's going to be all right, Tim."

There was the sound of the thump of a tail on the floor of the Jeep, and then that whimper of pain.

"It gets more and more confusing," Joey said. "It can't have anything to do with the other fires, can it?"

"You know anyone who'd want to set fire to my cabin, boy?"

"No. But anyway, they can't claim it was Fletch. He's in jail."

"If they're still believing in the accomplice theory, they'll be saying it was that accomplice," Uncle George said.

"That doesn't make sense, Uncle George. If Fletch was guilty, which of course he isn't, why would his accomplice want to hurt you? You're defending Fletch."

"I might be getting too close to someone who has to defend himself."

"But you're not getting close, are you?"

"I wish to God I was, Joey." Uncle George swept past a cruising car on the main road.

"What would he expect to gain by setting fire to your cabin?" Joey asked.

"Get me so concerned with my own problems that I'd stop looking for him," Uncle George said.

"But you're not looking for an accomplice because you don't believe there is an accomplice!"

Uncle George gave the boy a quick glance. "I'm looking for an arsonist and a murderer, Joey. We all know he exists."

"You got any leads to him, Uncle George?"

Uncle George looked ahead down the road. Dr. Kellog's office wasn't too far away. "I know some things about him, Joey. He's a man who had access to military fire bombs. I think he's a man who murdered another man, set a fire at the Harder farm to drag most of the town out there. Then he planted his victim in the Town Hall and set it on fire. Those fires were set almost twenty hours ago. The fire in my cabin was set only an hour ago. The man we want is still in Lakeview. He's among us, watching us, listening to us. He's decided I'm dangerous to him."

"Maybe he's just crazy enough to want to keep confusing people," Joey said.

Uncle George slowed down outside the white house that was Dr. Kellog's home, office, and animal clinic.

"Every murderer is crazy, Joey. Finding the answer to what makes him that way could get us to him."

Dr. Kellog, a young man new to Lakeview, handled Timmy gently when Uncle George and Joey got him inside.

"Knock him out while we examine the wound," Kellog said, giving the animal some kind of hypodermic injection. After a moment Timmy lay perfectly still. "You're lucky, Mr. Crowder. A few inches the other way and the bullet would have gone right through his heart."

"His chances?" Uncle George asked.

"Give me a little time, Mr. Crowder."

Uncle George stood to one side, watching the young vet touch Timmy's wound with a rubber-gloved hand.

"Bullet's there, all right," Kellog said. "I'll get it out as soon as he's all the way under."

The dog seemed to Uncle George to be frighteningly still before Dr. Kellog reached for a scalpel on his tray of instruments. It was painful to watch him cut into Timmy, but the dog didn't even quiver. It wasn't hurting him.

Dr. Kellog finally dug out the bullet, looked at it closely, and then tossed it in the air and caught it. "A low caliber slug. A .22 I'd guess. You'd expect a guy who throws fire bombs around to have a more powerful gun. This comes from something you might expect a kid to be carrying."

Uncle George didn't comment for a moment. He was remembering what Esther had said about the person she'd seen running from the south wing of the Town Hall. "A boy, small, agile, running like a deer."

Dr. Kellog turned away from Timmy. "I think we got lucky all around, Mr. Crowder. As far as I can tell, there's no major damage. He's lost a lot of blood, flesh in his right

67

shoulder pretty churned up, a small nick in his upper thigh bone, not serious."

"Can you give him some kind of transfusion?"

"In the big veterinary hospitals they often have a 'donor dog,'" Dr. Kellog said. "They go into shock from loss of blood and need something. I'll give Timmy what's called Lactated Ringer's. It should do the trick."

"Thanks for whatever."

"Leave him here overnight," Kellog said. "Check with me in the morning."

"I'll come in right after breakfast," Uncle George said. "Timmy will want to know that I haven't deserted him. Thank you, Doctor—thank you very much."

Back in the Jeep, Uncle George sat silent for a moment behind the wheel. Joey sat beside him, staring across the shopping center's parking lot at the lights in the windows of his parents' house. His mother would be anxious about what had happened up at the cabin.

"You heard what Doc Kellog said about a 'kid's weapon'?" Uncle George asked.

"Yeah!" Joey said. "Sure!"

"And you remember what your mom said about the boy who ran out of the south wing of the Town Hall after the third bomb went off?"

"Of course. That's what we were arguing with my dad about."

"You suppose, Joey, we've been way off base from the very start?"

"How do you mean?"

"We've all been looking for a man, full of hatred, with access to high explosives. The troopers settled right away on Fletch. I've been looking somewhere else. But none of us has been looking for kids in spite of what your mom told us."

"Oh, wow!"

68

"We know the woods are full of violent-minded kids from everything we see and read and hear. Vandalism is probably the number-one crime in the country today. We have kids like that here in Lakeview, don't we?"

"I guess so," Joey said after a moment. "Maybe a dozen or more who sort of gang together. But fire bombs, Uncle George?"

"Why not? If they're illegal, you can find someone selling them. Drugs are illegal. You can buy them. Handguns are illegal. You can buy them. Any kind of stolen goods are illegal. You can buy them. One of these Mafia-type kids comes across a carton of fire bombs and he has to use them in a spectacular way. The Harder farm—Seth Harder was a villain to lawless kids who'd heard the Fletch Johnson story. Everyone in town had heard it. The Town Hall represented authority. Blow it up! Later, I represented authority. Torch me."

"You're leaving out things, Uncle George. The dead man in the Town Hall."

Uncle George nodded. "You try to make things fit your current theory, whatever it is. Let's suppose, Joey. Let's suppose that man was a stranger, driving through town. He's right by the Town Hall when the bomb in the north wing goes off. He's heading toward the fire when the bomb in the center section goes off. He's headed for the south wing when he runs into your mom's young man. Identification. Our monster-kid pops him with his little .22, drags him into the south wing, and throws his third bomb. We can't find anyone who's missing because the man was from somewhere else and was heading somewhere else."

"He must have had a car," Joey said. "It would be parked where he left it, wouldn't it?"

"Not if our monster-kid took it and drove it away, dumped it somewhere. We could find it in the bottom of the lake tomorrow—or next year."

"But that's just 'supposing,' Uncle George."

"How close are you to this gang of tough kids, Joey? Could you listen to them talk, tell me what you hear?"

"They wouldn't talk in front of me," Joey said. He gave his uncle a twisted little smile. "You see, I'm a 'nice kid,' not to be trusted."

"We better check you in, boy," Uncle George said. "Your mom's probably heard the news and is worried."

Esther and Hector were in their living room. "I'd be out searching the town for you two if Red Egan hadn't called us," Esther said. "How is Timmy?"

"Doc Kellog is hopeful."

"How lucky your cabin didn't go, George."

"The gods were with us," Uncle George said. "Bob Reed and Timmy threw my visitor off schedule."

"There's one thing about you, Joey," Hector Trimble said. "When we don't know where you are, we can always be sure you're with the great George Crowder—somewhere you shouldn't be that's dangerous."

"Oh, Hector!" Esther said.

"Fires, murders, shootings!" Hector said.

"He's still very much in one piece, Hector," Esther said.

"No thanks to your brother!"

"I'll hand you the whip some other day, Hector," Uncle George said. "Right now I need some help from Esther." He outlined to his sister his latest notion about the gang of young toughs in town. "Has time brought you any closer to identifying the boy you saw running from the Town Hall, Es?"

Esther shook her head. "Just his back as he ran away," she said.

"Guess at how tall?"

"Not tall. Five-five, five-seven. Slight. Weight around a hundred and fifteen, a hundred and twenty pounds."

"Well, that's something. Dark hair, you said."

70

"Yes. Worn long. That is, down his neck a little like a lot of the boys do today."

"That ring any bell with you, Joey?"

Joey hesitated. "Two or three kids aren't as tall as I am," he said. "But none of them has dark hair the way Mom describes it."

"At night, with only the strange light from the fire—his hair could have shown up darker than it is."

"It was dark hair—black," Esther insisted. "The light was very bright, George. The whole place was in flames, you know."

It wasn't much. There was one other person who might be helpful, Uncle George thought. Marilyn Stroud, living just across the way, would know most of the kids in town, being Assistant Principal at the school. He said good night to the Trimbles, promising Joey he'd stop by for him when he went to see Timmy in the morning.

There were still lights on in Marilyn's cottage when he knocked on her front door. Marilyn wasn't alone when she opened the door to him. Mildred, Rich Nolan's wife, was there. She was a bright-eyed Irish woman in her mid-thirties who still looked like a handsome young girl.

"Good evening, Mrs. Nolan," he said.

"Mildred to you, George," the woman said.

"My pleasure," Uncle George said.

The two women had heard most of the news and there was a flood of questions and inquiries for Timmy before Uncle George could get around to his business.

"Ruby?" he asked.

"She and little Rod have turned in," Marilyn said. "It's been a rugged day for them. Mildred came over to repeat Rich's offer of the guest cottage at their place."

"And a little eating money," Mildred said. "Of course she'd be alone there. Alone but quite safe. I can understand why she wants to stay with Marilyn for a little, with

71

someone she knows and who cares for her. But the offer stands open."

"I'm sure she'll appreciate it in a day or two, Mildred. I have some questions I want to ask Marilyn which, you might say, I don't want to have made public."

"Where I grew up in Ireland, George, we lived with secrets every day," Mildred said. "You kept them if you didn't want your tongue cut out. If this has something to do with the problems here in town, Rich and I would help if we could."

"You've lived here for a lot of years now," Uncle George said. "You must have seen a lot of kids grow up."

Mildred's smile was bright and bitter. "And wished that some of them hadn't. We've been the target of a lot of vandalism since we came here—the rich strangers!"

"I don't want what I'm thinking to become public gossip."

"You can count on me, George," Mildred said. "Or I'll go, if that would make you happier."

It was a decision that had to be made then and Uncle George made it. He told the two women about his latest thinking. "I thought Marilyn could give me a list of who the bad kids might be. Perhaps pick out one who might fit Esther's description."

"Goodness, George, I need a minute or two to think," Marilyn said.

"When I mentioned vandalism," Mildred Nolan said, "I was talking about dirty words painted on the fence, a dog I had chained up unchained, vegetables stolen out of our kitchen garden, air let out of tires. Nothing as bad as fires or a bodily attack on anyone."

"Someone suddenly running wild."

"But murder?"

"Seth Harder's death is second-degree murder under the

law," Uncle George said. "Not premeditated, but the result of a criminal act. The man in the Town Hall could be the same thing. He fell asleep in a corner somewhere and woke up too late. Or it could be something else." He outlined his notion to the two women about a stranger passing through, stopping and going to the burning Town Hall to offer help, coming face-to-face with the fire bomber, and being shot with the .22 caliber gun or pistol. "That would be first degree."

"But the motive in the first place?" Mildred asked. "If it isn't Fletch Johnson, and I have to say the evidence is pretty strong—"

"He couldn't have set fire to the Town Hall. He was under arrest. Couldn't have set fire to my place for the same reason."

"You don't buy the accomplice theory, George?" Mildred asked.

"No, I don't, but I have to admit there's someone working full time out there—the Town Hall, arson, and murder; the bombs in Fletch Johnson's truck; the fire at my place and what may still be the murder of my dog!" His mouth twisted but it wasn't a smile. "At the start of this I was looking for justice and truth. Right now I'm more concerned with revenge on the scum who hurt Timmy."

"But the motive for all this, George? It can't be just for excitement, can it?"

"I won't say 'can't be,'" Uncle George said. "My own feeling is that the key to this thing lies in the Town Hall. I keep telling myself that the Harder fire was set to draw the townspeople away from where the action really was—the Town Hall. I think the fire at my place was intended to involve me so completely that I'd stop trying to draw the troopers' attention away from Fletch Johnson, steer them somewhere else . . ."

"But the original motive that started it all," Mildred persisted. "The Town Hall, whatever went on there?"

Uncle George shrugged. "Bad kids may just have wanted to attack authority—spelled with a capital A. Stranger wanting to help gets in the way, is shot, and burned to ashes along with the building. Second possibility is that the man was killed or rendered unconscious, planted in the building, which was torched in the hope no one would ever know he'd existed."

"Those fire bombs make it almost certain they were prepared in advance, don't they?" Mildred asked. "You don't kill a man, hide his body, and go out in the middle of a New England summer night hoping to buy illegal explosives."

"You're pretty sharp at this kind of thing, Mildred," Uncle George said.

"God help me, I grew up with this kind of thing all around me."

Marilyn Stroud joined them from her desk, where she'd been making notes of some sort.

"I've got a list of names here for you, George," she said. "These are fourteen kids whom I'd call the bad ones, the town toughs, the Junior Mafia." She handed the paper to Uncle George. "There are three who just wouldn't fit Esther's description—first there's Eddie Mitchum. He's over six feet tall, broad shoulders, blond hair. He's only fifteen, but looked at from behind, running away, you'd have to think he was a grown man. There's Blinky Morris. He's short, but he weighs over two hundred pounds. Nothing 'agile' or 'deerlike' about Blinky. Finally, there's Lou Tobin. He was born with a deformed foot—which probably accounts for his bitterness against the world in general. But Esther couldn't have seen him running anywhere. He can't run."

74

"The rest of the names—is there someone you'd call a leader?"

Marilyn smiled. "You won't believe it, but the real tough guy in that group is Tiny Watson."

"Paul Watson's kid?"

Marilyn nodded. "Smaller than his friends, always trying to show them that being little doesn't prevent him from being the toughest of them all. He's been trying to out-tough them ever since kindergarten. Now he's eighth grade and king of the walk."

"As I remember him, he has pretty fair hair," Uncle George said.

"I've been thinking, George," Marilyn said. "The boy Esther saw could have been wearing some kind of knitted cap, a stocking cap. In the bright, but uncertain and un-familiar light, Es might have thought she was seeing hair when it was really some kind of cap."

"So where would you start if you were I, Marilyn?" Uncle George asked.

"If I were you I wouldn't start, George. You're the law, you're their enemy. You need someone on your side they'll enjoy boasting to."

"What about you, Marilyn? You know these kids. They probably trust you."

Marilyn's smile was wry. "I'm the law, too, George. Vice Principal of their school. But there is someone—Ruby. She taught them during their early years at the school. She broke the rules by getting pregnant. The law—the school board—fired her. Her father threatened the next guy she cared for with a gun and warned him out of town. Ruby, they'd think, is one of them, persecuted by the rules, the law, the people in authority. If they have anything to boast about, they might boast to her."

"You think she'd try?" Uncle George asked.

"Ask her in the morning, George. Come by for breakfast. She's just about had it tonight. But I think she'll agree, when she understands she would be helping Fletch."

There were lights on in his cabin when Uncle George got there. No Timmy to greet him, but the truck parked outside spelled "friend." Red Egan was sitting opposite the TV set watching a late movie.

"Thought it was best not to leave your place unwatched," he said, as he leaned forward and turned off the set. "Your friend, whoever he is, might come back if he saw the coast was clear. Timmy?"

"Kellog thinks his chances are fair," Uncle George said. "Could you stand a slug of bourbon?"

"I have to make a confession," Red said. "I already helped myself."

Uncle George poured himself a drink from a bottle in the sideboard, added a splash of cold spring water from the sink.

When he rejoined Red, he handed him the list of names Marilyn had given him, explaining his newest theory to Red. "You must know most of those kids," he said.

"Know them? Every damn one of them has been through my office at one time or another," Red said. "If you'd asked me yesterday, I'd have said the worst expected of them was a kind of mean mischief."

"That's not what we're talking about tonight, Red."

"I know." The sheriff reached for the glass on the table beside him and took a healthy swallow of the drink he'd made himself. "One thing bothers me about your theory, George."

"Oh?"

"Those fire bombs. Six of them in a carton, right from the manufacturer. You have any idea what they're worth, George?"

"Not really."

"Couple of hundred bucks apiece, according to Sergeant Terry. Black market. Where would these kids get that kind of money? They don't have it. They don't have friends or family who'd buy them for them."

"So they stole 'em," Uncle George said.

"From where? You know anyone who'd have twelve- or fifteen-hundred-dollars worth of fire bombs—just in case?"

"Someone passing through town, stops at the lunchroom for something to eat. Kids see a stranger's car, rip it off while he's eating, go off with the fire bombs."

"And the guy doesn't complain when he finds them gone?"

"Maybe not if he'd have to explain where he got them," Uncle George said.

"At least you've invented answers to back up your theory," Red said.

"Once the kids have the bombs—a lucky piece of thievery—they start having big ideas about a sensational way to make use of them. The Town Hall, number one symbol of authority in Lakeview, is their target. That will really have Authority crying. They torch Harder's place . . ."

"Why Harder's?"

"Mean old man who mistreated his daughter," Uncle George said. "But mainly because it would draw everyone out of town so they could attack their main target."

"But someone got in the way?"

"Or was accidentally just sleeping there."

"It's a fascinating story, but you've got nothing to go to court with, George."

"I know," Uncle George said. "But if Ruby Harder will help us in the morning, she might get some kind of lead for us."

"Let us pray," Red said. "But whoever it is, is right here somewhere, George. He'd be a long way from here, not torching your cabin, if he didn't belong here. He can't leave town because if he does, we might suddenly get ideas."

"And if it's a gang of kids, they'll all supply an alibi for each other."

"Maybe we can make it make more sense when we've slept on it. Mind if I stay here? At least we can take turns sleeping that way."

"If Timmy were here to warn me, I wouldn't need you. But stay, friend."

2

The beauty of enlisting Ruby Harder to deal with Tiny Watson and his gang was that she could approach them quite directly, ask for their special kind of help. What was the underground gossip? What were the rumors? They'd be willing to help Ruby because, in the first place, they liked her as a teacher when they were younger, and second, because she was the victim of self-righteous persecution, as they imagined they were.

"Of course I'll help if it will contribute to clearing Fletch," Ruby told Uncle George over breakfast coffee and eggs at Marilyn Stroud's. "But you have to realize, Mr. Crowder, that if they're in any way involved with the fires and the dead man in the Town Hall, there won't be a whisper of it. Their lips will be frozen shut. If they're not involved, they'll tell me what they know, or think, or guess, but it may take days for anything to come out that's useful. That may be too late."

"To stop more violence, you mean? I guess the people of Lakeview could stand a few hours of peace. One thing's certain, Ruby. This man, if he's local, isn't going any place. To turn up missing would be like a confession."

Marilyn's front doorbell sounded. It was Rich and Mildred Nolan.

"I promised to keep your secret, George," Mildred said, "but I don't think that included my husband."

"It's safe with me, Mr. Crowder," Rich said. He glanced at Ruby. "This young lady agreed to help?"

"I've agreed to do what I can," Ruby said. "But as I've just been saying to Mr. Crowder, it could take time."

"That's why Mildred and I came over," Rich said. "We thought we might help speed things up."

"How?" Uncle George asked.

"A reward," Rich said. "A substantial reward. Twenty-five thousand dollars for information leading to the arrest and conviction of the man responsible for the fires and two deaths. That ought to be enough to whet somebody's appetite, don't you think?"

"Especially those greedy kids," Marilyn said. "It might make them a little more eager to help Purdy."

"You might wind up having to pay it," Uncle George said.

"You ought to know better than anyone, Mr. Crowder, how easily I can afford it," Rich Nolan said. "My father, when he was on a spree, might have tipped a hatcheck girl that much."

"It certainly couldn't hurt," Uncle George said. "Get it on the radio right away. I think you can still make this week's paper. Signs in public places. First of all, put the money in the bank so if anyone asks, they'll know it's for real."

"Anything else we can do?" Rich asked. He looked at Ruby. "That guest cottage is still yours, young lady."

"I don't think I should accept while I'm trying to deal with Tiny Watson and his gang," Ruby said. "They might think your place was 'the wrong side of the tracks,' Mr. Nolan."

"So, the offer still stays open," Mildred said.

The word about a twenty-five thousand dollar reward was already circulating before Uncle George reached the police barracks, having stopped on the way to cheer up Timmy.

"That should at least get a few more people on our team," Captain Purdy said. He, Red Egan, Tom Andrews, the local newspaper editor, and Carl Carpenter, the County Attorney, were holding a council of war when Uncle George joined them.

"You're to thank for the reward, I guess, George," Tom Andrews said.

"Thank the young man with a big heart," Uncle George said.

"And a deep pocketbook," Carpenter said. "Going to cost him a hundred and fifty grand for his share of rebuilding. That's not hay!"

"His old man really piled it up for him," Purdy said. "We have something for you, George, that seems to support one of your theories."

"Oh?"

"The State Police lab has been sifting through some ashes, particularly those around where the burned body was found in the Town Hall."

"A lead to his identity?"

Purdy shook his head. "A little blob of melted lead," he said. "They think it may be a bullet."

"A .22?"

"No way to tell, now or ever," Purdy said. "But it supports the idea that the man who died there had been shot."

"Which makes you a genius, Crowder," Carpenter said. "Except that Doc Walters can't prove he was shot, and that blob of lead could have come off a light fixture, or something in somebody's desk, or any one of a hundred things. I know you'll keep pedaling your particular bicycle, but it doesn't convince me of anything—except that it was hot as hell in there when that guy burned up."

Perhaps if Carpenter's attitude wasn't so hostile, Uncle George might have told them all then and there about Ruby Harder's involvement. He decided to save it for later for Red Egan. Carpenter could take it, drag in Tiny Watson and his gang for questioning, and spoil any chance Ruby had to come up with something real.

The worst thing about the situation at the moment, Uncle George told himself, was that there was no clear trail to follow. Hunt a killer animal in the woods and there'll be paw marks, broken branches in the brush, possibly blood-stains if there's been a fight. Whatever trail the arsonist-murderer had left here in Lakeview had been consumed by the fires he'd set. Of course there was another kind of trail, a psychological trail, a trail of past human relationships. That was why Purdy and Carpenter and some of the other lawmen were so eager to make Fletch Johnson prove out as the villain. They had his name, they had his background, which labeled him a kind of expert in the world of fire bombs, they had his quarrel with Seth Harder and their threats and counterthreats. Why look for anything else when all those facts made an almost perfect case? Almost because Fletch could not have thrown the Town Hall bombs and he couldn't have made the attempt to torch Uncle George's cabin. Accomplice? Not the smallest clue, not the faintest lead. Concentrating on Fletch Johnson and a myth-ical accomplice was a dangerous waste of time. If there was a lead anywhere, the man responsible for the fires and murders was being given ample time to obliterate it.

Timmy, according to Dr. Kellog, looked this morning as though he was going to make it. At the animal clinic, the big red dog had stirred out of what looked like an almost

81

comatose sleep to give a little cry of delight at the sight of his master, and to indulge in contented whimpers as Uncle George sat beside him and stroked his head.

"A few days," Kellog said. "I won't say he'll be as good as new—that leg will bother him for quite a while—but he'll be able to go home with you."

"He could be important to me," Uncle George said. "Not just as a friend. I cherish his companionship. But if he ever encounters the person who broke into my place and shot him, he'll let me know just as clearly as if he spoke English."

Area radio was already holding out the enticement of a reward in five figures. Nobody in the area was talking about anything but the chance to cash in. Something that Uncle George knew would happen did happen. People had seen fifty or sixty strangers in town the day and night before, all suspicious! Uncle George tried a few people he thought wouldn't have dollar signs replacing the pupils in their eyes. He was still playing with two ideas—the stranger who ran to help out at the fire and was shot for his pains, and the man who was eating lunch at a local place and had a carton of fire bombs stolen from his car.

A dead blank from all reliable sources. Tony Spaulding, proprietor of the local diner, had nothing to offer. His was a favorite place for truckers on the road. Most of them were familiar, almost friends. The day of the fire there'd been no one he didn't know. With the news now on national radio and TV, as well as the area stations, if any of those truckers were missing, someone would almost certainly have been on the phone to the cops by now.

Lawson Baxtor, proprietor of the local gas station, had nothing. Most of the strangers who stopped at his place were salesmen. "Looking for where some of the rich people live, like the Foster Graveses, or Dennis Cooney, or the

Nolans. You can smell the vacuum cleaners in the trunks of their cars."

"Anybody the day before the fire?"

"Not that I remember, but there could have been someone who asked one of the kids who work for me. I'll check."

As he turned away from the garage owner, he saw a man standing by his Jeep. He knew the man, and yet he didn't know him, couldn't put a name on him. The man's smile was cheerful as Uncle George approached him.

"You're George Crowder?"

"Yes." Uncle George shook his head. "I know you but I don't know you."

"You watch the news on network television?"

"Oh, for God's sake!" Uncle George said. "You're Dan Lewis!" Dan Lewis rated with the great newsmen on TV. He was in almost every home in the United States, just before or just after your suppertime, depending on your time zone. Uncle George knew him but didn't know him because he'd never seen him in the flesh before.

Lewis held out his hand. "Andrews, your local newspaper editor, tells me you're the man I need to help me put my *Tonight Show* together—for tonight!" Lewis's handshake was firm; his direct blue eyes instilled an instant confidence in him.

"Pleasure to meet you, Mr. Lewis," Uncle George said. "I've been following you for a good many years."

"I hope with pleasure," Lewis said.

"With confidence, at least, that I wasn't being sold a bill of goods," Uncle George said. "How often is the news pleasant these days?"

"You're right, of course, Mr. Crowder. That's why I'm here. To cover your unpleasant news, which will be interesting the whole country from coast to coast by tonight. I need to present Lakeview as it is, not dream up something.

Andrews says you were born here, raised here, became a part of the legal machinery for a number of years, and now, retired, are admired, respected, and on a first-name basis with almost everyone in the community."

"Andrews tell you why I retired?"

"Yes."

"No comment?"

Lewis shrugged. "You prosecuted a man on the basis of evidence supplied by the State Police. That evidence didn't hold up after it was too late. No one then or now holds you responsible for what went wrong."

"Someday let's talk about it," Uncle George said. "Right now is not a time for remembering the past. Some kind of demented terrorist is threatening this town. I'm one of the people looking for him."

"You know where to look?"

"Frankly, no. Andrews probably told you that I'm defending Fletcher Johnson, the man the police have arrested."

"You must believe in your client's innocence," Lewis said. "You're not going to get rich defending an out-of-work farmhand." Lewis's eyes brightened. "Or is the town's good fairy footing the bill? A hundred and fifty grand to rebuild the Town Hall, twenty-five thousand in reward money. Paying Johnson's legal fees wouldn't be out of character."

"Rich Nolan?"

"I didn't have my own show ten years or more ago when it happened," Lewis said. "Irish rebel inherits millions from a long lost father, gives up the cause, and settles down in New England to become a country squire. I understand you were involved in that, too, Mr. Crowder."

"I drew up Pat Nolan's will. I was gone by the time Rich Nolan surfaced. He is not, incidentally, paying me anything to defend Fletch Johnson."

"You believe in Johnson?"

84

"I know what he couldn't have done. I'm not worried about what's going to happen to him because he couldn't have torched the Town Hall or my place."

"The accomplice theory?" Lewis asked.

"I won't believe it until somebody can point at someone."

"Well, maybe I can be of some help," Lewis said. "I'm going to do my *Tonight Show* from the lobby of the Lakeview Inn. We'll be featuring the Lakeview story tonight and tomorrow. Millions of people will be watching. Maybe someone will decide they want to go public before that kind of audience. But I particularly want you, Mr. Crowder."

"On the air?"

Lewis nodded. "You'll create a picture of what this town is really like. Working on the case, you'll have intelligent and articulate answers to questions. Can you be at the Inn at six o'clock? Give us time to discuss what's at the top of the list by tonight. Go on the air at seven."

"I don't know what the day is going to produce, Mr. Lewis," Uncle George said. "I can see how your show might be helpful, but I can't promise to be anywhere at any specific time. If a clear trail shows up somewhere, I'll be following it."

"I'll take what I can get," Lewis said. "But I'll need you, Mr. Crowder. I don't want to blow things by talking out of the wrong side of my mouth in front of a few million people."

It was a frustrating day because there were no handles to hang onto. There was no hope of hearing anything from Ruby Harder until she'd had a chance to ingratiate herself with the "bad kids." No one had seen a stranger in town at the time of the Town Hall fire. It had been about midnight, but the town had been awake—all headed for or concentrating on the Harder fire. A stranger could have driven into town unnoticed, stopped his car, gone to the Town Hall blaze, and been seen only by a killer.

Carl Carpenter, the County Attorney, took time off in the middle of the day to be interviewed on the area radio. He assured his listeners that the next time they heard from him, he'd have an open-and-shut case "against an arsonist-murderer and his accomplice, despite what I'm sure will be a brilliant effort to make us look somewhere else by a local hero, Uncle George Crowder." His tone of voice made it clear how little respect he had for Uncle George.

Uncle George himself talked to probably fifty people he thought might help, know something about who Fletch Johnson's friends might be, who might know anything about black-market operators selling any kind of illegal goods in the area. Nothing but a great big zero for a day's work.

About five-thirty, Uncle George went to his cabin, changed into a tweed jacket that would look a little better on TV than his work clothes, and drove back into town. He stopped at Marilyn Stroud's. Ruby Harder wasn't there but she'd phoned in.

"She knows you're going to be on the Dan Lewis *Tonight Show*," Marilyn said. "It's been on every commercial announcement on TV all day. If you'll come back here after the show, George, she'll let you know if the day has produced for her."

"Sound like she had something?"

"She said some of the boys had talked to her, but nothing that helps, except that they all agree with you that Fletch Johnson isn't It."

"What I need is who it is, not who it isn't," Uncle George said.

He headed across town to the Inn. The parking lot was jammed with cars and the handsome lobby was crowded to

86

the walls with people who wanted to be an audience for the famous *Tonight Show*.

Captain Purdy was there, obviously invited by Lewis to be another guest.

"It could help, I suppose," he said when Uncle George joined him. "From the look of you, you haven't turned up a miracle."

"Nothing."

"Between you and me—same here," Purdy said. He pointed to the end of the room where microphones and cameras had been set up. "That redheaded guy over there is Babe Fallon. He's the producer of the show. Better let him know you're here."

Uncle George glanced at his watch. It was almost twenty past six. "I don't see Lewis. He wanted to talk before air time."

"He hasn't shown up yet," Purdy said. "I don't imagine you'll get stage fright, George, if you have to go on without preparation."

Uncle George wedged his way through people, all of whom wanted to ask him questions, to where Fallon stood, talking to one of the cameramen.

"Mr. Crowder? Thanks for coming."

"I said 'maybe,' but I made it," Uncle George said.

"Dan's late, but he should be here any minute," Fallon said. "You got any bombshells to give us?"

"Nothing I didn't have this morning when I talked to Lewis," Uncle George said. "Can I stay up here by the cameras? I'll be talked to death by that crowd out there."

"Sure. You'll be stationed by that first microphone on the left when we go." He glanced at his wristwatch, frowning. "It's not like Dan to stretch it this thin when he has guests to prepare."

"Maybe he's got onto something," Uncle George said. "None of the rest of us have been that lucky."

"I've been producing this show for nine and a half years for Dan," Fallon said. "He's been on the air for ten. As far as I know he's never been late for a weekday show in all that time. It's his life. Promptness is his golden rule."

A quarter to seven and no Dan Lewis.

Fallon got Uncle George and Captain Purdy together at the back of the area where the show was to go on. He was obviously worried. "He hasn't called. We're supposed to go on in twelve minutes. If he'd been in a car accident or something, wouldn't your people have let us know?" he asked Captain Purdy.

"Yes, if they knew who he was. If he knew who he was. If he was hurt and couldn't tell them—" Purdy suggested.

"Would they know President Reagan if they found him in an accident? Come on, Captain, Dan's is one of the best-known faces in America. They've known all day he was going to be here."

"George and I could answer questions if there's anyone else to ask them."

"The people don't want to see anyone else but Dan, unless we have a story about him to tell them."

At seven o'clock Babe Fallon went to one of the mikes. The cameras blinked little red lights. "This is Babe Fallon, Dan Lewis's producer. For some reason Dan has not appeared for his show. And so I return you now to our New York studios."

For the first time in ten years, Dan Lewis had failed to appear for his weekday *Tonight Show*. America was suddenly more interested in that than the Lakeview tragedies.

As far as the world apart from Lakeview was concerned, it was as if a Dan Rather, or a Walter Cronkite, or even a Johnny Carson had suddenly disappeared into a dark pool of violence. Dan Lewis was their nightly friend, their guide and counselor in a world of politics, and war, and terrorism.

Dan Lewis had a family—his second wife Laura and a twelve-year-old son, Jason, who was at a boys' camp somewhere in New York State. Laura Lewis sounded concerned when she was reached on the phone. She had been waiting for Dan's show to come on and, like the rest of America, had heard that he wasn't going to appear for the broadcast. She hadn't begun to worry yet. No, she hadn't heard from Dan—not yet.

It was unthinkable, according to Babe Fallon and some higher-ups from the network's New York office, that Lewis could have voluntarily missed a show. It was hard for any of them to imagine that he could have left the Lakeview area. The story he was going to cover that night was there.

"Of course," someone in New York suggested, "Dan is a first-rate reporter, when you come right down to it. If he came onto some kind of clue or lead, it could have persuaded him to follow someone or something—somewhere."

He'd driven to Lakeview in his own car, a cream-colored Mercedes-Benz with a thin, scarlet stripe around the body. It wasn't an unnoticeable car. His license plate had his initials DL and the number 051 on it. People had seen it earlier in the day, parked outside the Inn where Lewis and Babe Fallon were making arrangements for that night's broadcast. Where he went or when he left, no one had a clue, until Rich and Mildred Nolan turned up at the Inn a little after eight, looking for Captain Purdy. Uncle George was still there, waiting for something to turn up that would set him into motion. The Nolans, like most of America, had heard the news about the missed broadcast.

"As a matter of fact we were listening, waiting for it to come on," Rich Nolan told Captain Purdy and Uncle George. "Announcement came that Lewis hadn't shown. We were surprised because he'd been at our place this afternoon to ask us to be on the show—the rebuilding of the Town Hall, the reward, all that."

"And you said 'no'?" Purdy asked. "Because you weren't here when the time came."

"We said 'no' because we thought it would look as if we were trying to get some kind of personal publicity for what we're trying to do for the town."

"Rich isn't doing what he's doing to get a halo," Mildred said. "He's just doing what he thinks his father would want him to do with what was once his father's money."

"There is one thing I guess you should know," Rich Nolan said. "I had met Dan Lewis eleven or so years ago—before my father died, before I inherited his estate."

"You've been friends all that time?" Purdy asked.

"I said I met him," Rich said. "In Ireland—Dublin. He was part of a news team for the network that came over there to film a special on the trouble there. Lewis interviewed me—I was one of the people involved in the trouble—and I never saw him again, except on television, until this afternoon."

"He came out to your house just to ask you to be on tonight's show?" Purdy asked.

"He reminded Rich that they'd met before," Mildred said.

"'Met' is the only word for it," Rich said. "That time, back in Ireland, Lewis was just one of a team of reporters. I was introduced to him but I couldn't have told you his name an hour later. Of course, when Mildred and I came to settle here, we began to look at television, caught the *Tonight Show*, and I realized that Dan Lewis had been one of that team of reporters back in Dublin."

"So much for ancient history," Purdy said. "What time this afternoon did Lewis come out to your place?"

Rich Nolan glanced at his wife. "I guess it was around three o'clock, wasn't it, Milly?"

"It was a couple of minutes past three," Mildred Nolan said. "I was working in my flower garden, saw this un-

90

familiar car drive in. I remember glancing at my watch because it seemed early for a social call. Then I thought it must be someone about the rebuilding project, or the reward. Then he got close and I saw it was Dan Lewis. I'd been watching him almost every night for the last nine years or more. I introduced myself and he told me why he'd come—to get us to go on his show that night."

"About then I came out of the house and joined them," Rich Nolan said. "We sat down in some garden chairs and talked."

"About your going on his show?"

"Yes, and about the general situation here in Lakeview."

"General situation?"

"Two fires and an attempt at a third one; two deaths and a wounded dog."

"Did Lewis express any opinions?" Purdy asked.

"He said he couldn't allow himself to take sides until all possibilities had been heard. He said he had you, Captain Purdy, who leaned toward the idea that Fletcher Johnson and an accomplice were guilty. You, Mr. Crowder, who believed it had to be someone else and were going to act as Johnson's lawyer. He was going to try to get two noninvolved local citizens to express their opinions; and Mildred and I were to talk about what was being planned to repair the damage; and bring someone forward who knows something with regard to the reward. All of this didn't take more than ten or twelve minutes, Captain."

"Did Lewis tell you where he was going when he left you?" Purdy asked.

"No," Rich Nolan said. "I don't think he did, did he, Milly?"

"No. I'm sure he didn't."

"But you saw him leave? Which way did he head?"

"You know our place, Captain," Rich Nolan said. "We were up by the front door garden. The driveway winds down to the stone gates that open onto the main road. We can't see those gates from the house. Lewis got in his car, waved good-bye, tooted his horn, and took off. There's no way we could see whether he headed back toward town when he went through the gates, or headed the other way."

Purdy looked at Uncle George. "Anything you'd like to ask, George?"

Uncle George drew a deep breath. "Lewis was obviously trying to line up the guests for his show," he said. "He'd already talked to Purdy and me. He didn't tell you who the 'uninvolved' people he was after were?"

"No."

"Didn't ask for your advice?"

"No."

"Didn't ask you how to get to so-and-so's house?"

"No."

"He was a stranger here in town," Uncle George persisted. "He wouldn't know how to get to one place from another without asking. We'll probably come up with someone he asked for directions to your place."

"He didn't ask us about anyone. He just took off," Mildred said.

"Isn't it likely he would have asked Tom Andrews for information like that?" Rich asked. "One news medium to another, he from network, Tom the local newspaper editor?"

"Sounds logical," Uncle George said. "We'll try Tom. But Lewis didn't hint to you that he was onto something, had a strong feeling about someone?"

"Not to me," Rich said.

"All the conversation about Lakeview began after Rich joined us," Mildred said. "When I first introduced myself as he came up the path from his car, there was just small talk—I chattering about having enjoyed him on television,

92

he saying that Rich and I seemed to gravitate toward violence, years ago back in Ireland, now here in Lakeview."

Uncle George glanced at Purdy. "It looks as if Lewis wasn't playing detective, just trying to line up people for his show."

"Then he's the only person in town who isn't trying to play detective," Purdy said.

"He's a professional," Uncle George said. "His job was to get an interesting show on the air at seven o'clock."

"But he didn't show up for it himself," Purdy said.

If Ruby Harder had learned anything about Tiny Watson's "bad kids," she must have it by now. Still without a faint glimmer of light from anywhere, Uncle George headed across the village green to Marilyn Stroud's cottage. Ruby Harder was there, looking exhausted. She was sitting at Marilyn's kitchen table with a mug of coffee and the remnants of some kind of sandwich.

"I wish I had something solid for you, Mr. Crowder," she said.

"Rod all right?" Uncle George asked.

"Two-year-olds are sound asleep by nine o'clock, Mr. Crowder."

It was just after nine, Uncle George realized. Dan Lewis had been missing for at least three hours. "You know about Dan Lewis?"

Both women nodded. "Another thing Fletch couldn't be involved with from his jail cell," Ruby said. "Doesn't that help him, Mr. Crowder?"

Uncle George's mouth moved in a bitter little twist. "Some smart guy like Carl Carpenter is going to come up with a new idea," he said. "He'll twist it around to Fletch being the accomplice who provided the fire bombs and set the fire at your place. The main man, whom we've been thinking of as the accomplice, torched the Town Hall, tried to burn me out, and has now done something to Dan Lewis."

"They just won't look for new facts," Marilyn said.

"I have to concede they're not easy to come by," Uncle George said. "Want to tell me about you, Ruby?"

The girl sipped at her coffee, put down the china mug, and leaned back in her chair. "I've got allies, but no facts," she said. "I got lucky. When I left Marilyn's to look for kids, I ran into Tiny Watson just across the street. He's the little king of the mob, you know. It turned out he was looking for me, had been waiting for me to come out of Marilyn's house."

"If he wanted you, why didn't he come knock on the door and ask for you?"

"Marilyn is the 'enemy,' Vice Principal of the school," Ruby said, smiling at Marilyn. "So he took me to what he called 'our clubhouse.' It's an old abandoned shed back of his father's lumberyard. There wasn't anybody there but I could see what it's used for; ashtrays for cigarette smoking, maybe marijuana, centerfold pictures from magazines like *Playboy*, some weights for exercising. I'd already asked him what he wanted from me. Tiny told me he and his pals wanted to find a way they could help Fletch."

"You believed that?"

"When you've been a teacher, Mr. Crowder, you can make a pretty accurate guess when a kid is lying to you and when he's telling the truth. I thought Tiny was telling me the truth and I could ask him some questions."

"Like?"

"First of all, why did he want to help Fletch." Ruby's smile was a tired one. "Well, it wasn't because they love Fletch. It was because they hated my father for what he did to Fletch, because they hate the State Police, and they hate Carl Carpenter, the County Attorney. In their book the bad

94

guys were doing an injustice to someone who had to be a good guy."

"'Had to be'?" Uncle George asked.

"The 'bad guys' are against him so he has to be a 'good guy,'" Ruby said.

"That's the kind of logic we're getting from everywhere," Uncle George said.

"More practically, I asked Tiny what the talk was in town," Ruby said. "Ninety percent against Fletch, Tiny told me. Mostly because there isn't anyone else to suspect. And there were the fire bombs in his truck."

"You asked him about fire bombs?" Uncle George asked.

Ruby nodded. "He said he and his pals didn't even know such things existed, certainly not that they were available anywhere nearby." The bitter little twist of Ruby's lips wasn't a smile. "If he'd known about fire bombs and that they could be had, he and his gang would have been interested. His words were that they could 'sure have raised hell with the bad guys' if they'd known about them and how to get them."

"Did you ask him where they were at the time of the fires?"

"It was nearly midnight when our place went up," Ruby said. "Tiny and his gang all have families here in town. They're supposed to be in and accounted for at that time of night. They don't circulate as a gang at that time. The State Police have an eye open for them. I suppose we could find out by checking each family and account for most of them. But when the siren went off for the fire at our place, they were all up and gone. You'd have to chain them down to keep them away from excitement."

"They must have talked together later."

"They did, of course. A couple of them saw Fletch out at the farm, trying to get Rod and me away from danger. Later, a couple of them saw the State Police arrest Fletch."

Ruby's laugh was mirthless. "Right away they were Fletch's friends."

"Nothing beforehand that suggested trouble was coming?" Uncle George asked.

"Tiny says no. Of course they'd all heard about the quarrel between my father and Fletch. They'd all been waiting to see how Fletch would get even."

"And they thought the fire was it?"

"I'm sorry to say, Mr. Crowder, that they're not for Fletch because they don't think he did it, but because they think he was justified."

"Not the best kind of allies, are they?" Uncle George said.

"They think if anyone can get Fletch off it's you, Mr. Crowder. So you're a 'good guy.' I think they'd talk to you if they thought it was helping Fletch."

"I can't lose by trying," Uncle George said. "I still don't have any other starting point."

Marilyn's phone rang and she answered it. "Oh, hello, Red. Yes, he's right here." She held out the phone to Uncle George. "Red for you. He sounds a little wound up."

Uncle George took the phone. "Yes, Red?"

"They've found Dan Lewis," Red said.

"Oh, great. Where was he?"

"In the old marble quarry down at the south end of the lake."

Uncle George frowned. "I don't get it. In the quarry?"

"That cream-colored Mercedes was in the quarry, and Lewis was in the Mercedes," Red said.

"Look, start over, will you, Red!"

"Lewis was in the car."

"Drowned?"

"Maybe. But he was shot right between the eyes before he hit the water. They say it's a small caliber bullet, like the one that nicked Timmy."

96

"You can't drive into that quarry by accident, Red!"

"I know. Someone who knew about the old quarry road had to drive the car up there, or force Lewis to drive it up there. You better get down here to the barracks, George. At least this is another one your client can't be responsible for. He hasn't escaped." Red sounded bitter. "Someone took the trouble to check."

3

The eyes of the world would be focused on Lakeview now. Dan Lewis, famous television newsman, murdered, would bring the press from everywhere to this small New England village, plus the FBI, probably private detectives hired by the network, and an army of curiosity seekers. A couple of fires and what may well have been a couple of accidental deaths would take a back seat to a giant manhunt for the killer of Dan Lewis. It was already on television before Uncle George left Marilyn Stroud's cottage.

Uncle George knew the countryside down where Lewis had been found like the back of his hand. As a kid he and his peers had used the old abandoned quarry, fed by fresh springs, as a private swimming pool. It was well off the main road. You could skinny-dip there without being caught at it. The quarry hadn't been used as a source of marble for more than fifty years, and the road to it, once surfaced with crushed stone, was a mass of weeds and short brush. There was no way in the world that a stranger like Dan Lewis could have driven up there by accident. And why would he have wanted to go up there? And how had he been found there at nine o'clock at night?

The story had a rather comic and titillating twist to it for local people. It was a beautiful moonlit night. Some of the young people, Tiny Watson's gang and others, still used the old quarry as a private swimming hole. On this night, some of the boys had gone up there, accompanied by several girls. There was to be a little naked dipping, which would be a village scandal for the next week or so. A couple, boy and girl, stripped of their clothes, had made the first dive in together, with nearly serious results. The cream-colored Mercedes was nose-down in the pool, just below the surface. The boy actually banged his head on the rear bumper.

A couple of the boys dove down and spotted Dan Lewis behind the wheel of the car, held in place by a seat belt. They had no idea at the time who it was, but they knew it wasn't anyone local because of the New York license plate— DL 051. The minute one of the kids phoned the State Police barracks, the cops knew who it was. They'd been looking for that license plate for the best part of an hour.

There was no way to get the car up in a hurry, but a couple of scuba divers went down, got the car door open, cut the seat belt, and dragged Dan Lewis out. The ambulance crew went through the motions of trying to revive Lewis, but they knew it was hopeless. The bullet wound just above the bridge of Lewis's nose had written period to his life-span.

"What the hell was Dan Lewis doing up there at the old quarry?" Captain Purdy asked. Uncle George, who had just arrived, and Red Egan were his audience, but actually he was asking anyone in the world who could provide him with an answer.

"Somebody had to have told him there was something for him to see," Red Egan said.

"Or not be seen," Uncle George said. "Someone who didn't want to be seen talking to Dan Lewis."

"And Lewis just drove over the edge of the quarry and dove down in?" Purdy asked.

"Maybe after somebody shot him," Uncle George said. "He wasn't there alone, Jim."

Purdy nodded, scowling. "Doc Walters says he couldn't have driven the car any distance after he was shot."

"Except into the quarry," Red Egan said.

"After turning off his lights," Captain Purdy said.

"Let's try to make sense as we go along, Jim," Uncle George said. "It was still daylight, we assume, when he went into the quarry. People were already looking for him at seven o'clock."

The door to Purdy's office opened and Dr. Walters was admitted by a trooper who was standing guard outside. The old doctor looked done in. "You going to produce any more bodies for me today, Jim, I've gone fishing!" He sat down beside Purdy's desk and rubbed at his eyes with the knuckles of his hands. Then he looked up. "First of all—officially—the gunshot killed him. There's water in his lungs, but it got there after he'd stopped breathing. And—officially—the bullet is a twin of the one they took out of your dog, George. I don't mean just another .22. The two bullets have gone to the state lab for a ballistics report. But I can tell you what it will be. Under my microscope they show exactly the same whirls and grooves. Not the slightest doubt they were fired from the same gun. Ballistics will be able to tell you whether it was a rifle or a handgun. If there's anything else I can help you with, ask me quick!"

"What was found on him?" Purdy asked.

"What you'd expect—wallet containing a driver's license, half a dozen credit cards, some blank checks on a New York bank. Glasses in a case and a ballpoint pen on the inside pocket of his jacket. One outside pocket had a notebook. Carpenter has it so I can't tell you what was in it. Other outside pocket a pipe and a Zippo lighter. Pants pockets, rear—a handkerchief in one, a roll-up tobacco pouch in the other. In the front pockets—the left one about a hundred

99

and thirty dollars in bills, and less than a dollar in change in the other, along with what looks like house keys. His car keys are, I suppose, in the car."

"How did that notebook get turned over to Carpenter?" Uncle George asked.

"Jim's boss gave it to him," the doctor said.

"Your boss?" Uncle George asked Purdy.

Purdy nodded. "State Commander, Captain Sam Corbett. Big name suddenly involved, top brass on the scene."

"But that notebook would be evidence."

"So the County Attorney's got it," Purdy said. "But I saw it. Fallon says Dan Lewis had a crate full of little cheap notebooks. He used a new one each day just for that day's broadcast. Then it would be put aside as a record of who he'd talked to, where he'd gotten material he'd used on that particular show. This one has Tom Andrews's name. That's where we thought he'd go, one newsman to another. Me, you, George, the Nolans, Foster Graves, four or five others—people he'd hoped to get on the show tonight or tomorrow night. That's all. Andrews tells us Lewis got those names from him, actually saw him write them down in that notebook. Routine, perfectly normal procedure according to Fallon."

"I'd like to go home," Dr. Walters said.

"Go, Doc," Purdy said.

The doctor pushed himself up with a little groan, as if every bone in his body ached. "Of course, if you need me—" he said and walked stiffly out.

"So we're sitting here to accomplish what?" Uncle George asked.

"Wrecking crew is trying to pull Lewis's car up out of the quarry," Purdy said. "When we can examine it, we may find out who was with Lewis, who steered him up there to the quarry."

Uncle George turned toward the door. "I don't sit very well," he said. "I'm going to find some of the kids who were

100

out there swimming. They might have something that would help."

"You won't get anything out of those little bastards," Purdy said.

Uncle George smiled. "Of course they won't talk to cops," he said. "But I'm a good guy, defending an innocent man who's being persecuted by those cops. Remember?"

Paul Watson's lumberyard was at the south end of town, stacks of lumber and prepared logs for cabins. In the daytime the busy sound of power saws was perpetual. It was after eleven at night when Uncle George got out there. He was pleased to see lights burning in the windows of Paul Watson's house. The whole town had seemed to be awake as he drove down the main street. Lakeview had been transformed into a place of terror, with the whole world watching.

Paul Watson answered Uncle George's knock on the front door. He was a middle-aged man, almost totally bald, with a cheerful face that was almost always wreathed in a "welcome, customer" smile. This night he opened the door, unsmiling, with a rifle cradled in his arms.

"George Crowder!" he said, obviously surprised.

"Sorry to barge in on you so late," Uncle George said, "but I saw your lights."

"Watching television, like everyone else in town," Watson said.

"Your boy here, Paul?"

"Oh, brother! What's he been up to now?"

"He hasn't been up to anything that I know of. But I thought he might be able to tell me something about what went on out at the quarry tonight. Ruby Harder tells me Tiny isn't unfriendly."

"He wasn't out there," Watson said.

"But he must have heard a dozen accounts of what happened from friends of his who were."

"Come in," Watson said. "I'll call him."

You live in a small town, circulate in the stores and on the village green, and you see dozens of people every day that you say hello to but don't really know. Paul Watson, a widower, and his fifteen-year-old son were two such people in Uncle George's life.

The boy who came down the stairs in answer to his father's summons was short, slender, very intense looking, his bright blue eyes suspicious and defensive. He was wearing a dark blue flannel bathrobe over a pair of white pajamas.

"Mr. Crowder wants to talk to you, Mort," Watson said.

Uncle George recalled that the boy's first name was Mortimer, though all his friends called him Tiny. "Sorry to get you up, boy," he said.

"I wasn't asleep. Watching the television like everyone else, I guess. I've got one up in my room," the boy said.

"You like to be called Mort or Tiny?" Uncle George asked.

"My friends call me Tiny," the boy said.

"Miss Ruby tells me you could be helpful to me if you wanted."

"I'd be willing to help Fletch Johnson if I could," Tiny said.

"Anything that will stop what's going on here in town will help Fletch," Uncle George said. "If you've been watching television, you know that Dan Lewis, the *Tonight Show* man, is dead, trapped in his car in the old marble quarry, shot in the head."

Tiny nodded.

"You may or may not have heard that he was shot with the same gun that was used to shoot my dog, Timmy."

"Oh, wow!" the boy said. "I hadn't heard that."

"Were you with those kids out at the quarry who found him?" Uncle George asked.

Tiny glanced at his father, looked down at his bare toes,

and then back at Uncle George. "I suppose someone told you I was. I told my father I wasn't, because I thought it would make trouble—naked girls and all that."

"Damn you, Mort!" Paul Watson said. "Will you never learn to trust me?"

"There's no crime in his having been out there, Paul," Uncle George said. "Kids have been swimming out there since I was ten years old."

"Naked girls!" Paul Watson muttered.

"That's not what I'm interested in, at least, not just now," Uncle George said, smiling at the boy.

"We go to the quarry," Tiny said, "because the only other place is the town beach. All the rest of the lakefront is private, a rich man here, his rich neighbor next to him, all around the lake. At the town beach they have a lifeguard, and a sort of town manager watching every move you make."

"Naked girls!" Paul Watson said again.

"What time did you all go up there?" Uncle George asked.

"A little before seven o'clock," Tiny said.

"Broad daylight," Uncle George said. "It doesn't get dark with daylight saving time till after eight. You notice anything as you walked up?"

"Like what?"

"Like a car had recently driven up?"

"We weren't looking for anything, we didn't notice anything," Tiny said.

"How many of you were there?"

"Twelve, I think—eight guys and four girls."

"Naked!" Paul Watson said.

Uncle George grinned at him. "They haven't got their clothes off yet, Paul. Give them time!"

"It was a sort of 'last one in's a rotten egg' situation," Tiny said. "We all started to undress. One guy and one girl were the first. They dove in at the top. If you remember, Mr.

103

Crowder, it's about six feet down to the water on the top side, steep little dive. We were all screeching and yelling and then Fred Brainerd surfaced. He was the first guy in, and he was waving his arms and shouting. I could see blood on his forehead. He was yelling at us that there was a car in there. He'd struck his head on the bumper. I was only down to my shorts, but I dove in to have a look. I didn't have the wind to go down any deeper than to see the back end of the car. It was standing right on its nose. Another of the kids had a scuba mask and he went down far enough to see that was a man strapped in the driver's seat. We couldn't do anything about it. One of the kids ran to the nearest house, the Foster Graves place, and used the phone to call the State Police. They came. I suppose it was about a half an hour from the time we first got there."

"Around seven thirty?"

"I imagine."

"And then?"

"Some divers went down and got the man out, and we heard it was Dan Lewis," Tiny said.

"There must have been a lot of talk, Tiny. Anyone suggest why Dan Lewis would have gone up to the quarry?"

"He was shot," Tiny said. "Either someone forced him to drive up there, shot him, and let the car take a dive, or he was shot, driven up there, strapped into the driver's seat, and the car pushed in."

"If they know it was a .22 gun, it shouldn't be hard to find out who has a license for one here in town," Paul Watson said. "Person who owns it must be local. Your dog was shot yesterday, wasn't he?"

"I bet there are a thousand unlicensed guns in this town, Paul. Most people think they're entitled to have a weapon with which to protect their own property."

"No way to check it, anyway," Tiny said. "Records like that all went up in the Town Hall fire."

"Tiny, will you stay in touch with me, let me know if you

104

hear any gossip that might be useful to me?" Uncle George asked.

"Sure. But it looks pretty good for Fletch, doesn't it? He couldn't have done this."

"You heard the theory that he had an accomplice?"

"That's bull!" Tiny said.

"Now they're suggesting that Fletch was somebody's accomplice," Uncle George said. "Supplied the bombs for him, probably set the first fire."

"And framed himself by leaving two bombs in his own truck to be found by the cops?" Tiny asked. "How crazy can those cops get?"

"Not half as crazy as whoever's terrorizing our town, Tiny," Uncle George said.

Captain Sam Corbett, in command of the entire State Police force, had not been sent to Lakeview just to make the department look good when a national figure was murdered in their jurisdiction. Corbett was a former FBI man whose specialty was homicide, and in today's world that seems to go hand in hand with terrorism. Corbett hadn't been sent to Lakeview to take over from Captain Purdy, but to add to Purdy's firepower in a case the whole country would be watching.

In his Jeep on his way back into town from the Watson place, Uncle George was flagged down by a State Police car, blinking lights on its roof, its siren sending people running to their windows. Some new violence?

"Captain Corbett's been trying to find you, Mr. Crowder. You weren't at your cabin. Captain Purdy thought you might be at Miss Stroud's, but she told us you'd gone out to Watson's lumberyard. Watson told us you'd just left. I've been watching for you."

"Something new?"

"I don't know. Corbett and Purdy are at the Inn. If you wouldn't mind stopping there—"

Captain Corbett wasn't someone you'd have chosen to lead the charge of the Light Brigade. Slim, almost frail looking, his talents, Uncle George thought, must be cerebral and not physical. His cold, gray eyes looked sharp enough to read the label on the inside of your shirt collar.

"Grateful to you for dropping by so late in the evening, Mr. Crowder," Corbett said. His voice was soft, almost a gentle purr, but Uncle George guessed the captain could give that a biting edge if he chose.

"I've been running around in circles all day," Uncle George said. "Another stop here is just part of a route that doesn't seem to be going anywhere."

Purdy nodded in agreement. The three men were in what was the Inn manager's office. "I told Corbett you can read the woods as easily as a kid can handle *McGuffey's Reader*," he said.

"If you're talking about the marble quarry, I can tell you what's there to read without even looking," Uncle George said. "Trampled over by a herd of elephants! First the kids who went swimming and found Lewis in his car, underwater. Then the first troopers who came, then the ambulance and its crew, then Doc Walters's car, then another army of troopers, then a few hundred curiosity seekers, looking for whatever there might be to see. If you can read anything out of that mess, Captain Corbett, you'd have to be psychic."

"Even if he left a calling card, it would be pretty hard to find," Purdy said.

"Calling card?"

"A clear footprint, an empty cigarette pack, a button or a piece of cloth torn off his jacket—"

Uncle George agreed. "Trampled out of sight—at least until morning when we can have a look at it in bright sunlight."

"The County Attorney is probably up in his hotel room

106

soaking his head," Corbett said. "He's got a man locked up who probably set the first fire and caused the death of Seth Harder, but that man couldn't have done any of the rest of these things. We haven't got a whiff of an accomplice, Carpenter's theory."

"Except the fire bombs that were found in Fletch Johnson's truck," Purdy said. "Same kind of bomb that was used on the Harder farm and later on the Town Hall. Hard to say there's no connection."

Corbett glanced at Uncle George. "As Johnson's lawyer—"

"You want to talk to me as Fletch Johnson's lawyer," Uncle George cut in, "or as a man who has had a long experience with crime and people with criminal motives?"

"Either or both," Corbett said. "I know you're not an ambulance chaser trying to make a reputation for yourself by defending Johnson. As a matter of fact, several people have told me, including Captain Purdy here, that I'd be well advised to sit at your feet and listen."

"Flattery will get you nothing in this case," Uncle George said.

"So let's put together what we do have," Corbett said.

"I'll do the listening, because I don't have anything to contribute," Uncle George said.

"Interrupt me if I get off base," Corbett said. He leaned back in his chair, making church steeples with his fingers. "The Harder fire and the Town Hall fire were set in the middle of the night. Early hours of the morning, you could say. The next night the attempt is made on your cabin, Mr. Crowder. So what do we have? A man who does not leave town, probably local, who uses darkness to shield his criminal activities."

"But—"

"I know, Mr. Crowder—a great big *but*. Dan Lewis left the Nolans' house about three-thirty in the afternoon. His dead body was found in his car, submerged in the quarry,

107

less than a mile from the Nolans', at around seven o'clock. Bright sunny day every bit of that time. What does that tell us?"

"That he doesn't need darkness," Purdy said.

"It confirms that he's local," Uncle George said. "He can move around in the daylight without attracting attention. Normal for him to be seen around. Also, the quarry spells 'local.' Only someone local would know that that old, abandoned road leads to a place where he could dump a body and a car."

"So he kills a man, dumps him and his car into the quarry, goes back down the road to the main highway, and hitchhikes a ride back to town."

"Or just goes to where he left his own car," Corbett said.

"Or went up the hill back of the quarry, down the other side, and there he is in town," Uncle George said.

"If he went that way, could you follow his trail, Crowder?"

Uncle George shrugged. "We could try in daylight."

Corbett twisted in his chair. "Ever since I got here, everyone I've talked to keeps referring to 'this man' who's done all these things. Yet one of the very first pieces of testimony you had, Purdy, was Crowder's sister, Mrs. Trimble. She saw a 'boy' running away from the Town Hall fire. How come nobody talks about a kid or kids."

"Way ahead of you, Captain," Uncle George said. "I'd just come from talking to a kid when your trooper flagged me down. Ruby Harder has been following that kid lead all afternoon. The boy I talked with, Tiny Watson, is one of the ones who was in the swimming party at the quarry."

"The Watson gang!" Purdy said.

"I'd take an oath Tiny Watson doesn't know anything, but he may come up with something later if you don't harass him."

"Surely we should question him," Corbett said.

"Let him alone. He thinks I'm his friend, at least Fletch

108

Johnson's friend. Put the heat on him and you've lost someone who could be useful."

"Tiny Watson won't squeal on one of his own," Purdy said. "Never has, never will."

"Maybe it'll be different this time," Uncle George said. "Tiny thinks, and so do I, that somebody tried to frame Fletch Johnson by planting those fire bombs in his truck. Tiny and his friends are Fletch's friends at the moment."

"You're aware of one thing that nobody has even approached," Corbett said. "Why the attack on Dan Lewis? He'd only been in town a few hours, all of them daylight hours. He'd just been circulating in the center of town— here at the Inn, setting up; police barracks. Wouldn't know any back roads or trails. What could he have seen, or what information could he have picked up that has missed us? Our man or kid couldn't wait to let him go on the air with his *Tonight Show*. He had to be silenced before that."

"Or it has no connection with our crimes? Something private, personal, not related to our fires and threats," Purdy suggested.

"Something tells me not to buy that, Jim," Uncle George said.

"About the attempt on your place, Crowder," Corbett said, "the question I want to ask you is would your dog actually attack someone, bite them, if they were trespassing on your property?"

Uncle George frowned. "He's trained to warn me. If I wasn't there—I don't know. He might."

"Our man tried to get into your house to get it going from the inside." Corbett's smile was angry. "He'd run out of fire bombs, left them in Fletch Johnson's truck. If it's any comfort to you, Crowder, that suggests you weren't in his original plan, or he'd have saved one of them for you."

"With one of those bombs, my place would have burned to the ground in five minutes," Uncle George said.

"The place is locked. He recognizes the kind of lock—if

109

he can just reach inside he can open the front door easily. He knocks out a pane of glass, probably with the butt of his revolver. That stirs your dog and sets Bob Reed to shouting. He has to be quick. He reaches inside—and this is pure guesswork—your dog grabs his hand or wrist. He shoots to get himself free of the dog."

"He gets the door open," Purdy suggested, "tries to start his fire in the trash basket. Bob Reed is coming closer, shouting. He has to go."

"About the dog, Crowder—would he bite?"

"I've never known him to bite anyone," Uncle George said, "but under the conditions you describe, he might."

"It would be nice if he did," Corbett said, "because then we'd be looking for someone with a wounded hand."

The office door opened and a trooper stepped in. "The lady and Fallon are here," he said.

"Show them in," Purdy said. He turned to Uncle George. "Dan Lewis's wife—or widow. The network's flown her up here from New York."

Laura Lewis was a startlingly beautiful girl, obviously in shock. She was clinging to Babe Fallon's arm as though her life depended on it. Captain Purdy introduced himself, Corbett, and Uncle George.

"Do you know more than you did when I talked with you on the phone?" Her voice was unsteady, but a pleasant, rich contralto. Her golden blond hair hung down below her shoulders. She was city-dressed. Uncle George suddenly remembered that she was an actress—stage and screen, using her maiden name, Laura Stallings.

"I'm afraid not, Mrs. Lewis," Purdy said.

"I want to go to him," Laura Stallings-Lewis said. She probably expected people to call her by her stage name, Uncle George thought.

"The body is at the hospital," Purdy said. He must have

110

noticed the girl wince at the use of the word *body*. "I'm sorry, Mrs. Lewis, but we need to ask you a question or two before you leave here."

"What can Miss Stallings possibly tell you?" Fallon asked. "She'd never even heard of Lakeview until yesterday."

Protective friend, or more? Uncle George wondered.

"You knew your husband was coming here, Miss Stallings?" Corbett asked.

"Of course I knew, but only yesterday. I hadn't even heard of or read about the disasters here until Dan called me to tell me he was heading up here for two broadcasts—last night and tonight."

"He'd be away from home for two nights?"

"Being away from home for a night or two isn't—wasn't—unusual. Where the big news story is, is where Dan goes." The corners of her mouth twitched. There she was again, referring to things in the present when they were now in the past.

"Lakeview didn't ring any bells for you?" Corbett asked.

"Bells?"

"You'd never been here, ever talked about the town, had friends here?"

"No."

"But you'd heard your husband speak about the Nolans, Rich Nolan in particular?"

Laura Stallings shook her head. "Babe told me about the Nolans on the way here from the airport." Laura Stallings nodded toward Fallon, her husband's producer. "You have to understand, Captain, that Dan and I have only just celebrated our third anniversary." Her voice went out of control for a moment, but she was an actress and she knew how to regain command of it. "Dan's trip to Ireland was seven years or more before I even met him."

"He didn't mention having interviewed Nolan at the

111

time the Nolans came into all that money?" Corbett asked.

"That was at least ten years ago," Uncle George reminded him.

"So you didn't realize that your husband had a friend here in Lakeview, at least someone he knew from professional contact?"

"He didn't mention it to me," the girl said. "You understand, Dan called me from his office yesterday morning, to say he was coming up here to Lakeview for two broadcasts. We didn't have time for any gossip or talk about the story that was here. He just told me he'd be staying here at this Inn, gave me the phone number here, and that was that."

"That's all?" Corbett asked.

She looked away from him. "He—he told me he—loved me."

"I'm sorry, Miss Stallings. No matter where you step it hurts, I know." Corbett glanced at the other two men. "Anything you want to ask, Purdy, Crowder?"

"If Miss Stallings will be patient with me," Uncle George said.

"Please, I want to get to Dan—" the girl said.

"You also want the person who murdered him punished, don't you, Miss Stallings?"

"Of course. I'm sorry. It just seems to take forever—"

"The first thought everyone has had, quite naturally, is that what happened to your husband is definitely related to what's happened here, that he got a clue to something, a lead, and the terrorist had to stop him."

"What else?"

"It could be that it has nothing whatever to do with what's been happening here," Uncle George said. "Some grudge from the past, someone who thought he'd been injured by your husband's broadcasts. He lives in this area, possibly even this town. He hears your husband is coming here to do his *Tonight Show* in Lakeview. It's suddenly an ideal climate for revenge. Everyone will tie what happens to Dan Lewis to what's already happened in Lakeview. Do you recall anyone in this area who'd locked horns with your husband?"

Laura Stallings glanced at Fallon. They both looked puzzled.

"Dan just reported news and color background," Fallon said. "I don't ever recall his receiving threats, not from here or anywhere else. By the way, do you know who the dead man in the Town Hall was?"

"No way to identify him," Corbett said. "No one reported missing."

"Perhaps in the morning, Miss Stallings, when you've had a chance to get steadied, we could talk for a while about Dan Lewis. Something might come to you that is blotted out just now," Uncle George said.

"I don't know, Mr. Crowder. There are funeral arrangements to be made, thousands of phone calls, friends from all around the world."

"All wanting the same answer we want," Uncle George said. "Who?"

It was a strange feeling for Uncle George to head for his own house and feel a prickle along his spine that suggested danger. There was no Timmy to greet him or warn him of a hostile presence. There were no lights on in the cabin.

He drove his Jeep up close to the cabin, left the headlights on, and walked to the front door. There was no sign of anything as he unlocked the door and switched on the inside lights. Nothing disturbed, nothing out of place. He went back outside, turned off the Jeep headlights, and went back inside.

There hadn't been much chance to think about the attempt to burn him out. There'd been Timmy to take care of, Ruby Harder to enlist, and finally the incomprehensible murder of Dan Lewis. But why torch his cabin? He wasn't even close to fingering anyone. Early on he'd thought it was an attempt to distract him, to make certain that the case against Fletch Johnson went smoothly. Too much had happened now for anyone, with or without Uncle George's prompting, to believe that even if he were guilty, Fletch could have acted alone, something the killer couldn't have foreseen after the initial fires: the discovery of the dead man in the Town Hall.

A whole day had gone by with nothing much happening except that Uncle George had thrown some doubts on Fletch Johnson's guilt. By luck which had brought Bob Reed into the area to check his traps, and that had had Timmy on guard, the simple torching of the cabin had failed. But then the murder of a national figure by a man who obviously wasn't afraid to be seen around town in broad daylight—because he belonged there!

Uncle George had suggested to Laura Stallings that the earlier fires and deaths had nothing to do with the murder of her husband. Actually he didn't believe that for a moment. But it wasn't good enough to play a hunch. He had to prove that there was a connection beyond any doubt.

Sleep seemed impossible, and yet it came. When Uncle George woke, sunrise was showing in his east windows. The minute he opened his eyes, Uncle George found himself back in the center of the problem, his mind going full speed. It was as if he'd parked his car for a while, switched on the motor, and was ready to move. He found himself wakened by a question he hadn't asked before. What possible connection could there be between Dan Lewis and that bundle of charred bones found in the Town Hall? If this was all part of one pattern, then there had to be a connection. That connection, Uncle George told himself as he started to lather his face for an early shave, had to be from somewhere else. The whole town had been asking and there was no one

114

missing who might have been those burned remnants of a man. The whole wide world had been Dan Lewis's playground. Had he and "Mr. Bones" been linked in some way in that outer world? Could the killer have known that sooner or later Lewis would come up with an identification that would blow his ball game? But how could Lewis make such an identification? There was nothing left but ashes.

The music goes round and round—

Uncle George had just stepped out of the shower when he heard a banging on his front door. He pulled on a robe and went to answer it. It was a State Trooper named Wilson, whom he knew casually.

"They found the Watson boy, shot in the head. Down near the marble quarry where they found Dan Lewis."

"Shot in the head? Tiny Watson?"

"I guess the kids call him that," Trooper Wilson said. "His name is Mortimer. They think the bullet will match up with the one used on Dan Lewis—and your dog. Same gun!"

"The boy's condition?"

"Doc Walters says 'maybe,' but don't hope too much. He's in a coma. Hasn't been able to tell anyone anything. Corbett and Purdy know you were talking to the boy last night—only a few hours ago. Will you come down to the hospital? Corbett and Purdy are staying there in case the boy comes to."

"Of course I'll come," Uncle George said. "But the boy didn't tell me anything that'll help."

Part Three

1

An old phrase, "enough is too much," ran through Uncle George's mind as he left his Jeep in the hospital parking lot and went into the red brick building in search of Captain Purdy and company. In the space of forty-eight hours, Lakeview had accumulated three violent deaths plus the critical wounding of a boy and a dog. "Too much," any way you thought about it.

Purdy and Corbett were in a little waiting room adjoining the emergency room. With them was Paul Watson, Tiny's father, looking as though the world had come to a dead stop somewhere in orbit.

"Same gun," Purdy said. "Your dog, Dan Lewis, and now this boy. No question this time."

"How bad is it?" Uncle George asked.

"Bad," Purdy said. "He'd lost a lot of blood when they found him, but the real trouble is damage inside his head— probably brain damage."

"'They' found him? Who is 'they'?" Uncle George asked.

"Some of his friends; half a dozen boys and a girl. They'd gone back out to the quarry to see what there was to see, I guess. All of them had been in the swimming party the night before. Some of them, getting undressed when Lewis's car and body were discovered, may have left things behind. At any rate they found Tiny, carried him up the road to the Nolan place, and called for an ambulance."

"Nobody saw or heard anything?"

"No."

"Tiny hasn't made a sound or twitched a finger since they got him here," Purdy said. "Paul here says you were talking to Tiny just before midnight, George. We hoped perhaps he tipped you off to something helpful."

Uncle George shook his head slowly. "He talked to me in front of his father. Paul can tell you." He looked at Watson, who just nodded silently.

"Why did you go to talk to him, Crowder?" Captain Corbett asked.

"Just covering the remotest possibilities," Uncle George said. "I had a theory about maybe kids—my sister seeing a kid running from the Town Hall. Some kind of planned terrorism that got out of hand. Tiny was the head of a local gang. When you're as disoriented as we are, you cover all the territory."

"But the boy revealed nothing?" Corbett asked.

"Nothing."

"The last thing he said to me before he went to bed last night—after you'd gone, Crowder—was that it would be nice to pick up that twenty-five-thousand-dollar reward Mr. Nolan had posted. I told him to stay out of it, stay away from it. As usual he didn't pay any attention to me. When I got up for breakfast this morning, he'd already left the house. Playing detective!"

"And successfully, you have to believe," Corbett said.

"You have anything to prove that he was shot out there at the quarry?" Uncle George asked.

"That's where the other kids found him," Purdy said.

"That doesn't mean he was shot there, does it? He could have been carried there from somewhere else, couldn't he?"

"Why?"

Uncle George made an impatient gesture. "If you killed him, you wouldn't want him found on your front lawn,

120

would you? As a matter of fact, we don't know where Dan Lewis was shot. He didn't drive up to the quarry, voluntarily, to admire the view. And we don't know where the man in the Town Hall was shot."

"If he was shot," Corbett said.

"I'd make book on it, Captain," Uncle George said. "In my experience, a multiple killer follows the same pattern. Here we have three people shot, bodies moved. Suggest something to you, Corbett?"

"Your dog wasn't moved," Purdy said.

"Different circumstances," Uncle George said. "My dog didn't invade the killer's territory, wherever it is, and even if he had he couldn't tell what he saw."

"You might as well complete your invention, Crowder," Captain Corbett said.

"You can always have your turn, you know, Captain," Uncle George said, his smile sardonic. "I'm suggesting that three widely different people, probably not connected in any way, stumbled onto, wandered into, or were looking for and found, a place, or something in that place, that the killer couldn't afford to have revealed. Something that might reveal another crime that the killer had to keep hidden."

"Another murder?" Purdy asked, scowling.

"Not necessarily. But a crime," Uncle George said. "A crime the man will keep on killing, and killing, to keep covered."

"This place of yours where people are shot and then carted away from, must be very close by," Corbett said. "Dan Lewis's body, in his car, was found in the old marble quarry less than a mile from the place where he was last seen alive—the Nolans'."

"Last seen alive by anyone who's reported seeing him alive," Uncle George said.

121

"The Watson boy left his home on foot, according to his father." Corbett glanced at Watson.

Watson nodded. "Mort had smashed the front wheel on his bike. We'd been having an argument over whether I should have it fixed for him or whether he would have to earn the money to get it fixed. This morning he was without wheels."

"So he wasn't covering too great a distance from the Watson Lumber Company," Purdy said.

"So we don't know about the man in the Town Hall, how he got here or where he came from. But he came on whatever it is the murderer has to hide, which can't be too far away from the center of town," Uncle George said.

"You backing off your theory that the man in the Town Hall was a stranger passing through town, saw a fire, rushed in to help, and was shot when he came face to face with the arsonist?" Corbett asked.

"I'm at least throwing this one into the hat along with it," Uncle George said.

"What kind of a crime could three unconnected people stumble over, wander onto, or be looking for?" Purdy asked. "You make it sound like something you or I could run across by accident, know instantly that it was a crime and who committed it, and be shot on the spot. It's too far out, George. So let's get around to something real, like your conversation with Tiny Watson last night."

"There isn't much to tell," Uncle George said. "I'd had Ruby Harder working on him. She'd been his teacher once, and she was Fletch Johnson's girlfriend. She got Tiny ready to talk to me, but when he did, it was just an eyewitness account of what had already been reported to you—boys and girls going swimming."

"Naked!" Paul Watson said.

Uncle George ignored him. "Finding the car and Lewis's body strapped in it, notifying the cops, hanging around

122

while Lewis's body was removed, and later watching the wreckers pull the car up out of the water. I asked him if his gang knew anything, had heard anything, guessed at anything. Nothing. Guesses like ours."

"And yet he's up at daybreak looking for something," Corbett said.

Uncle George faced Corbett's cold blue stare deadpan. "You know how it is, Captain. There was a rich reward, the cops are a bunch of dummies, the smartest kid in town with his own mob should be able to find something if anyone can."

Corbett wasn't amused.

The door to the emergency room opened and Dr. Walters joined them. He looked like a man who'd been put through a meat grinder, literally and figuratively. There were some blood spots on the front of his green surgical robe.

"I'm afraid the news is bad, gentlemen," he said.

"Still unconscious?" Watson asked.

"I'm afraid he's gone, Paul. Never came around, never spoke a word."

"Oh, God!" Watson muttered, and turned away.

Only Corbett, to whom the Watsons were strangers, showed no emotional reaction. "I want every article of his clothing, especially his shoes, taken to the police lab," he said. "It's possible that his shoes might reveal some special kind of dirt or mud that would give us a clue to where he was walking." He glanced at Uncle George. "Your special crime spot, Crowder."

And so it was, officially, another murder. Uncle George had no doubt that ballistics would show that a bullet from the same gun that wounded Timmy and killed Dan Lewis had done in Tiny Watson. So what good did it do him to be sure of that? You had to find the gun and who owned it.

123

Uncle George decided to find Ruby Harder again and have her tell him which of Tiny Watson's gang would be likely to help him. He walked down through the main waiting room of the hospital, and found Rich and Mildred Nolan headed toward him.

"How is the boy?" Rich asked.

"He didn't make it," Uncle George said.

"How awful!" Mildred said.

"Was he able to tell them anything before—?" Rich let it hang there.

"Never spoke. Never said a word," Uncle George reported.

Rich shook his head. "There must be some kind of private detective, investigator, who could be helpful here, Mr. Crowder. We've got a killer running wild here. I don't know the Watsons, but they're neighbors, fellow townsmen. I'd foot the bill if I knew where to find the right man for the job."

"I think before you have your next cup of coffee, the FBI will be on the job. Thanks to Dan Lewis, this isn't local anymore. It's national."

"Please, please let us know if there's anything on earth we can do," Mildred said.

"Right now I'm headed to talk to some of Tiny's friends," Uncle George said. "Perhaps later you'd be willing to talk about Dan Lewis's visit with you. Some casual remark he might have made about where he'd been or where he was going."

"I don't remember any small talk like that," Rich said. "He was with us such a short time. It was all about years ago, our first meeting."

"Something may come to you later," Uncle George said. "Something that seemed unimportant at the time that could be vital."

"We'll try to remember if there was anything," Mildred said. "Come anytime you want, Mr. Crowder."

Uncle George went from sadness at the hospital to outrage and anger at Marilyn Stroud's. Most of Tiny Watson's friends were there with Ruby Harder, waiting for news. When Uncle George's Jeep pulled up outside the cottage the kids, boys and girls, came running down the path to surround him.

Fred Brainerd, the boy who'd dived into the quarry and struck his head on the bumper of Dan Lewis's car, asked the key question. "How is he, Mr. Crowder?"

"I'm sorry to have to tell you that he didn't make it," Uncle George said.

"Damn!" Brainerd said and slapped his forehead, in spite of the piece of tape that covered his wound.

A girl, whose name Uncle George knew—Sandra Witt—made a choking, sobbing sound. A sudden wave of profanity swept the group of kids.

"Was he able to tell them—?" Ruby Harder asked from the outer rim of the crowd.

"Never regained consciousness," Uncle George said.

"Damn! Damn! Damn!" Brainerd was beside himself.

"Did he talk to you this morning, any of you, before he took off?" Uncle George asked.

Everyone looked at everyone but nobody spoke.

"We don't usually get together that early in the day," Fred Brainerd said, finally. "We all got chores to do."

"I'm trying to find out where it happened," Uncle George said.

"Where it happened? They found him at the quarry, didn't they?"

"They found him there, but is that where he was shot? They found Dan Lewis there, but is that where he was shot? I have a feeling that Tiny, and Dan Lewis, and the man in the Town Hall all touched the same base, some-where else."

"But why would he move them—the killer? They were going to be found anyway," Fred Brainerd said.

"The killer didn't want attention attracted to some other place," Uncle George said. "Now if we could find out where Tiny was headed when he left the lumberyard this morning—"

"South end of town," one of the boys said. "He'd have to be headed north unless he was going off into the woods."

"Somewhere there are people who were up as early as Tiny—probably five-thirty or six in the morning. If you guys have the patience to go from house to house asking," Uncle George said, "we just might get a lead as to where he was headed, to where it happened, what he saw that he couldn't be allowed to talk about."

"We'll take the whole damn town apart, piece by piece," Fred said. "And I promise you, Mr. Crowder, when we find the son of a bitch who did Tiny in, I will personally take pleasure in cutting off—" He stopped to take a quick glance at Ruby Harder. "—cutting off his you-know-what."

"Let me know if you get anything solid," Uncle George said. "I don't know where I'll be, but you all know my Jeep when you see it."

The kids reminded Uncle George of the old Stephen Leacock character who "dashed off in all directions at once." Uncle George found himself deserted by everyone but Ruby Harder.

"I feel so guilty," the girl said, in an unsteady voice.

"Guilty?"

"I stirred up Tiny's interest, persuaded him to get in-volved, persuaded him to talk to you. Perhaps if I hadn't done that he wouldn't—"

"Nonsense," Uncle George interrupted, almost sharply. "If anything got him involved, like a few dozen other people in town, it is the reward Rich Nolan offered. To a fifteen-year-old boy, twenty-five thousand dollars looks like a fortune."

Ruby gave him a shaky smile. "Isn't it?" she asked.

"I suppose, especially if you owe it," Uncle George said. Rumor had it that Seth Harder had been perpetually in debt, trying to keep his dairy farm alive. "The thing that worries me is that, with all these would-be detectives at work, someone else will stumble across this forbidden place that cost Tiny, and Dan Lewis, and the man in the Town Hall their lives."

"What kind of place could it possibly be, Mr. Crowder? Right here in our village?"

"There's an old saying," Uncle George said, "about knowing where the bodies are buried. There's something somewhere that would reveal something about some crime that we haven't even a clue to yet. The trouble is, you and I and the kids are the only ones really looking. The troopers don't think much of it as an idea. You get the slightest hint of what it might be, Ruby, don't tell anyone else. Come straight to me."

"That doesn't include Miss Stroud, does it?"

"Marilyn, anyone," Uncle George said. "The minute there is someone else who knows, another name is added to the killer's hit list."

Across the village green Uncle George saw Red Egan's hatchback parked outside his sister's house. He drove the Jeep over there, parked, and went to the front door. Across the alley he could see Hector Trimble through the plate glass window of the pharmacy. Hector wasn't someone he wanted to spend time with that morning.

Esther opened the door to him and he saw his friend, Red, behind her in the living room.

"Joey?" Uncle George asked.

"He went down the street to Dr. Kellog's to check on how Timmy is," Esther said.

"Did he know about Tiny Watson?"

Esther's face clouded. "He knew that Tiny's been shot. He didn't know the latest."

"He does by now," Red Egan said. "Everybody in town's got their radios on. You're a hard guy to find, George."

"Oh?"

"Corbett told me your theory about some place people might stumble on by accident that would unmask our killer. I think you've almost got him convinced. I know you have me."

"That's nice, but it doesn't help unless you come up with a notion about where or what," Uncle George said. "I came here because I was worried about Joey, Esther."

"Why?"

"Half the kids in town are looking for that 'someplace.' I don't want Joey looking for it on his own. It would be like him."

"But why not?" Esther asked.

"Because he might find it," Uncle George said. "Stop and think what happened to other people who did."

"Oh, my God, George!"

"I don't want to scare you, Es, but I want you to understand and make Joey understand that it's not safe to try to play this out by himself. If he wanted to join up with Tiny Watson's gang it might be safer, but safest of all would be to leave this to the cops. I'm going to stop by Doc Kellog's to check on Timmy myself, and I'll try to make some serious sense to Joey. But if I miss him, find him and talk to him, Es."

Uncle George and Red Egan walked out of the Trimble house together.

"One thing bothers me, George," Red said.

"You're lucky if it's only one thing."

128

"Figure of speech," Red said. "But we're assuming that the man in the Town Hall, Dan Lewis, and Tiny Watson all came across something that would incriminate the man we're after. If it's something lying around for anyone to see, why does the killer leave it there? Why doesn't he move it, hide it? He's had two nights to work in."

"It can't be moved for some reason."

"Then everyone in town will see it, sooner or later," Red said. "I just can't conceive of what it could be. Something invisible that three totally unrelated people—the Town Hall guy, Dan Lewis, and Tiny Watson—could see, and that we, standing next to them, can't see."

Uncle George gave his friend a steady look. "Let's say that the secret is that a certain lady has a mole on her breast," he said. "You don't know it, I don't know it—even though we're standing right next to her, talking to her. But the man in the Town Hall knew it. He tried to rape her. Dan Lewis knew it because he accidentally walked into the bathroom where she was in the tub. Tiny Watson knew it because he's a mischievous kid, a peeping tom, who was looking through her bedroom window when she was dressing or undressing."

"Interesting," Red said. "I'm sorry I didn't get to see the lady's bosom. But so what?"

"Just to suggest that what's at the bottom of this may not be a tangible thing—a body, a stolen thing, like jewels, or negotiable bonds, something concrete. The man in the Town Hall was equipped to recognize some criminal truth—something about a crime you and I don't even know took place. He had to be killed to keep him from talking, his body obliterated so that he can't in any way be connected with something here in Lakeview. Then Dan Lewis turns up here, a man who travels the world, knows people from all walks of life everywhere. He sees something or someone, a thing or a person who would be meaningless to

129

us, but for Lewis it takes the lid off a crime he mustn't be allowed to reveal."

"And a little monster, like Tiny Watson?"

"Snooping around where he doesn't belong," Uncle George said. "He sees or overhears something and is caught with his pants down! Has to be silenced."

"You're leaving out George Crowder," Red said. "Have you forgotten? Someone shot your dog and tried to set fire to your house."

"I think that was to be a diversion," Uncle George said. "Our Mr. X had it all set up to frame Fletch Johnson. I was getting in the way of that and had better be diverted. God knows I wasn't close, then or now, to what it's all about." Uncle George reached for his car keys. "I better find Joey and try to turn him off."

Red put a hand on his arm. "See those two boys crossing the street?"

Uncle George looked and saw two young people wearing blue jeans, sport shirts, hair worn longish. "Those two boys are girls," he said. "Hard to tell the difference from behind the way they dress these days."

"I know," Red said. "I wonder if we should ask Es—"

"Ask her what?"

"Whether the boy she saw running from the Town Hall fire could have been a girl," Red said.

Joey wasn't at Dr. Kellog's when Uncle George got there.

"Left just a few minutes ago," the vet said. "The news about his friend, Tiny Watson, came over the radio while he was here. He seemed to get all steamed up. He left a message for you, George. It doesn't make much sense."

"And it was?"

"I was to tell you he was 'working on the case of the drowned Mercedes,'" Kellog said.

"Crazy kid," Uncle George said. Long ago he and Joey

had played what they called "The Sherlock Holmes" game. Uncle George was Sherlock Holmes and Joey was Dr. Watson. Now Joey was playing Sherlock Holmes himself! "Did he say where he was going, Doc?"

Kellog shook his head. "Out into the wild blue yonder, like everyone else, I guess. Nobody has a real lead, do they George?"

"Not that I know of. How's my dog doing?"

"Fine. He's going to be lame for a while, need medication put on the wound a couple of times a day for a week. Outside of that, you can take him home now, and God knows that'll please him. I think he thought Joey was going to take him home and when he didn't, he just slumped down."

The dog's delight was touching, his tail waving like a sail in a hurricane. Uncle George had to help him into the Jeep, but he sat up on the front seat, as if to tell the world, "This is who I am and this is where I belong!"

Uncle George, with Timmy beside him, cruised around the village for a few minutes looking for Joey, but there was no sign of the boy. A couple of people he stopped to ask hadn't seen Joey either. Where would Sherlock Holmes head for if he'd just taken over the case? Why, to the scene of the crime, of course.

Uncle George headed out to the lake, drove along past the gates to the Nolan property, and turned off on the old road leading up to the quarry. Up at the quarry there was no sign of life. Uncle George sat in the Jeep, looking down at the pool where Dan Lewis's Mercedes had "drowned." There couldn't be anything up here of consequence to find. An army of police and volunteers had gone over every square inch of it, not once but several times.

"Mr. Crowder!"

Uncle George turned and saw Rich Nolan looking down at him from the high ground above the quarry.

"A gathering place for Crowders?" Rich asked, smiling.

"Meaning?"

"Your nephew, Joey Trimble, was here not too long ago."
Rich came down the bank and walked over to the Jeep. He
reached out and stroked Timmy's red nose. The dog licked
a finger. "He's coming along, I see."

"You say Joey was here?"

"Kids who come here on foot to swim cut across my
upper field," Rich said. "I don't object, told them it was
fine with me. It's the way Joey would come if he was
walking."

"And he came that way?"

Rich nodded. "I've had that unfortunate Watson kid on
my mind," he said. "I wondered if he'd come across my
field. I wasn't sure if the troopers had looked there for some
trace of him. So I came out to satisfy myself nothing had
been overlooked. While I was looking along both sides of
the path the kids have made, your nephew came along,
bright as a button." Rich laughed. "He told me he often
helped you with your cases, just wanted to have a look at
the quarry to see for himself."

"We've often played detective games," Uncle George
said, "but not for real!"

Rich Nolan's smile faded. "It didn't seem wise to me that
he should be out trying something on his own," he said.
"He could run into the same thing the Watson kid did—and
pay the same price."

"I know," Uncle George said. "That's why I'm looking for
him."

"It's just unbelievable what's been going on here," Rich
said. "You live here for years, peacefully, and suddenly the
whole place blows up in your face. Two destructive fires,
three murders, and that attempt on you that failed."

"Thanks to my friend here," Uncle George said, patting
Timmy. "And the very good luck that Bob Reed happened
to be nearby."

"I've been thinking," Rich said.

"Guessing, you mean?"

"Not exactly. But this is a strangely mixed-up, divided community. There are the local people who've lived here all their lives—like you, and your sister, and your nephew. And there are people like me. I lived the first twenty-five years of my life without even thinking of Lakeview. I lived in Ireland, brought up in the midst of all the violence there. Then my father died, recognized me as his heir. So I've been living here for the last ten years. But all my past, my history, is somewhere else."

"So?"

"I'm only one of many like that, Mr. Crowder. Foster Graves, who owns the next place down the lake, was a criminal lawyer, practicing in New York. He retired five or six years ago, bought his house here, became a member of this community. But his history is somewhere else. And there are probably dozens more people like Graves and me, people who bought property here for a retirement time of life, or like me, inherited from parents. We think of them as belonging here but their pasts are all somewhere else."

"I think I see where you're headed," Uncle George said.

"A man who isn't local—I say he isn't because no one local has turned up missing—knows something about someone's past, maybe tried to blackmail that someone, and is killed. The fire is set at the Harder farm, which draws everyone out there, and then the murdered man is placed in the Town Hall and that's burned."

"Then this local man whose past is somewhere else tries to frame Fletch Johnson, I get in his way, and he plans to warn me off?"

"Something like that. Then Dan Lewis comes to town to do his *Tonight Show*. He didn't know anyone here in Lakeview except me," Rich said. "That's what he told Mildred and me. But his job, his work patterns, could have brought him into contact with any of the pasts of any of the

133

people whose histories lie somewhere else. He leaves our house, comes face to face with someone he knows from some other world, knows instantly who the killer and arsonist is, and is shot dead in his tracks."

"And the Watson boy?"

"It's not so easy to make sense out of that," Rich said. "But I have to believe that he saw something, heard something, and couldn't get away in time to tell anyone."

"What could he have seen or heard?"

"There's no way to guess at that until we can come up with someone who has something in his past, from another time, that he's got to keep hidden," Rich said. "The Watson boy couldn't have been looking for that something because he had no way of guessing it existed. He just came on it— and paid for that accidental discovery. It bothers me that the same thing could happen to your nephew, Mr. Crowder."

Uncle George sat silent, stroking Timmy's head.

"It bothers me," Rich said, "that all the troopers and experts are looking for some motive for all this here in town, when actually it can be almost anywhere else in the world."

Uncle George leaned forward and switched on the engine of his Jeep. "I'm going to keep trying to find Joey," he said. "But when this is all over, Rich, remind me to award you a gold star. For my money, your theory clears away a lot of fog."

What Rich Nolan had suggested was ingenious and quite probable, Uncle George thought as he drove down the old road from the quarry. But it opened up a kind of research that could take weeks, months. Probably twenty families would fall into the category of people whose pasts were in another place and time. Who could possibly dig out those histories in time to do anything about a killer, poised to strike again, right here in Lakeview, if he had to?

You couldn't find Joey by just driving around town, waiting for him to appear. If the boy was playing detective, he could be deliberately staying out of sight. Under other conditions, the big red setter might have been helpful. They had a game in which Joey would hide somewhere in the woods, then Uncle George would turn the dog loose with the command, "Find Joey!" Not possible now with his gimpy leg.

There didn't seem to be anything to do but keep circulating. On foot, Joey couldn't be very far away, but there was no reason to believe he was on foot. An ingratiating smile and the waggle of a thumb had been developed to a high art with most kids these days. Joey could have hitchhiked a ride to almost anywhere.

Still aimlessly circulating, Uncle George drove past the Lakeview Inn again and saw Babe Fallon, Dan Lewis's producer, talking to a strange man on the lawn, just off the Inn's front porch. A question he thought Fallon might be able to answer occurred to him and Uncle George pulled the Jeep into the Inn's front yard to park. He patted Timmy, said "Stay!" and walked over to Fallon and his companion.

"I'm glad to see you, Crowder. This is Steve Whitmore. You may know his work."

It was the same thing that had happened with Dan Lewis—a familiar stranger. Whitmore was another top newscaster from the network.

"I watched you broadcast the shuttle disaster from Florida, didn't I, Mr. Whitmore?" Uncle George asked. "As I remember, it was one of the longest nonstop broadcasts of all time—from about eleven-thirty in the morning until—"

"Till Dan Lewis took over on his *Tonight Show* at seven," Whitmore said. "But I wasn't unique. Dan Rather on CBS was among others who stayed with it all day."

"I was looking for you, Crowder, because we've decided to do the *Tonight Show* here tonight, with Steve anchoring it. Maybe tomorrow, too, if the case is still unsolved. We'd like you to be on the show. There'll be Captain Purdy, and the Nolans, the last people to see Dan alive."

"Except the man who killed him," Uncle George said. "I've just come from talking with Rich Nolan. He didn't mention the show."

"Because we haven't asked him yet," Fallon said. "Steve only just got here. I know they wouldn't go on with Dan, but this is different. This time they're directly involved, not just generous townspeople."

"Can we count on you, Mr. Crowder?" Whitmore asked.

"You ask me to commit myself to something hours from now," Uncle George said. "I can only say that I will if I can. Something hot breaks and who knows? How is Mrs. Lewis—Miss Stallings—bearing up?"

"As long as there are things for her to do, she's holding up fine," Fallon said. "There's going to come a time, probably after the funeral, when she'll break into a thousand pieces."

"She's a strong lady as long as she can be in action," Whitmore said.

Uncle George changed directions. "Rich Nolan came up with an interesting theory," he said. He explained Rich's notions about people who were thought of as local but whose pasts covered other times, other places. "His thought is that after Dan Lewis left him and his wife, he spotted someone who lit up a memory, and paid for that memory with his life."

"It sounds just a little weird to me," Whitmore said. "Dan leaves the Nolans, is driving along the road, sees someone he realizes is Jack the Ripper—from London— stops his car, says 'You're Jack the Ripper, aren't you?' and gets himself shot. Well, let me tell you, Crowder, Dan was a skilled reporter. In any situation like that he'd know the dangers, the risks. He'd have trailed the man until he got somewhere he could get help. Dan was never out to be a hero."

"I'm inclined to agree," Fallon said. "Dan wasn't a risk-taker unless it was the only way."

"So," Uncle George said, after a moment, "we don't know where Dan Lewis was headed when he left the Nolans. Maybe he came back here, encountered Jack the Ripper in the lobby."

Whitmore laughed. "So Dan points a finger at him and gets shot. In front of all the people milling around here, the Ripper carries his body out to the car, drives it off to the quarry—and on and on."

"So of course it didn't happen that way," Uncle George said. "But the two men pass in the lobby. Neither of them speaks but each of them knows what that meeting means to the other. Lewis heads for the phone in his room, is followed, and shot there. His body isn't moved until the coast is clear."

"But still in broad daylight," Fallon said. "He was found at the quarry in daylight."

Uncle George nodded. "Maybe we better start over," he said. "Tell me, gentlemen, Dan Lewis has been doing this show for about ten years?"

"Eleven years, three months," Fallon said. "I'd been with him a little over nine."

"Five days a week for eleven years and three months? No holidays?"

"He tried to plan a week off a couple of times a year. We'd film some specials along the way that could be used while he was away. He'd try to pick a stretch when there was a holiday, like Presidents' Day in February, or the Fourth of July. He'd do a historical special for those days. Some kind of specials for the other days—something on medical research, something on the space program, something that would be interesting at any time. Of course, if something tremendous happened in the news, he'd come back from wherever he was."

"Somewhere in storage are a mass of tapes. Five days a week, eleven years and three months."

Fallon laughed. "The network would have to buy up half of New York City to store all those tapes, and all the other tapes made by how many other reporters, dramatic people, musicians? There is a staff, Mr. Crowder, that goes over all those tapes. Where there is a tape with anything that sounds like an accusation—by the reporter, not some witness who appears who'd be subject to a lawsuit—but where the reporter might be subject. All the tapes, after a year or so—unless they have some sort of historical value—are destroyed."

"Historical value?"

"Like the assassination of a president, or a Martin Luther King, or a disaster like the explosion of the shuttle."

"They still have tapes from World War I," Uncle George said. "You mean it's a staff decision whether a tape is kept?"

"Or what portion of a tape is kept," Whitmore said. "I have sometimes forecast that the whole damn world is going to be strangled by tapes of its past."

"What's your interest in this, Crowder?" Fallon asked.

"Dan Lewis seeing something here that reminded him of his past; not *his* past, but his past reporting. It occurred to me that if tapes were available they might show someone from here, something that would tie up with someone from Lakeview."

Fallon shook his head. "If you have a lifetime to spend, Mr. Crowder."

"And, of course, I could come across it in the first hour!"

Rich Nolan's suggestion became a kind of obsession with Uncle George as the day wore on past noon. There was no sign of Joey and none of a dozen people who knew him well had seen him.

Someone whose past lay in another place and time? Rich

had mentioned the lawyer, Foster Graves, who owned the next property to his on the lake. Foster Graves had had a kind of Clarence Darrow reputation over the last fifty years in America. Uncle George had set him up as a kind of idol during his own adolescence and his early years in college and law school. The famous lawyer had no connection with Lakeview in those days. Uncle George had only seen him a couple of times on early newsreels at the movie theater, and later on television. It wasn't until after Uncle George had had his own disaster in the courts and disappeared from his own home and town that Foster Graves, retired, had bought the old Shelby estate on the lake and "became one of us."

When Uncle George returned to Lakeview from his self-imposed exile, he made a point of introducing himself to the older man. It became a casual but pleasant relationship; Uncle George in his early fifties, Graves in his early seventies. They talked about the law, mostly about notorious cases that were making the news. Graves, suffering from severe arthritis, couldn't join his younger friend in hunting or fishing, or any other physical relaxations, but they could talk together with pleasure and mutual respect. Uncle George felt he needed his older friend that day.

Foster Graves was sitting in a white iron armchair, just off the terrace of his lavish house overlooking the lake, enjoying the sunshine when Uncle George found him.

"Hallelujah!" Graves said, as Uncle George approached him. "Now I may hear something that makes sense!"

"Or total nonsense," Uncle George said, pulling up another iron chair to sit by his friend.

The old man wanted a complete rehash of what had been happening and what conclusions his younger friend had come to. Uncle George went over all the details. "Which add up to zero," he concluded.

"There's one strong possibility right at the starting gate,

139

George," the older man said. He had white hair, closely cropped, bushy white eyebrows that hung out over pale, but still bright blue eyes. "You're all assuming that the two fires, the attempt to torch your place, and three murders are all one piece."

"And at the starting gate—?"

"The fire at the Harder farm may have nothing whatever to do with the fire at the Town Hall. The Harder fire may have been just what everybody thought it was when they were fighting it, an act of revenge by your client, this Johnson fellow, against Seth Harder."

"The fire bombs? Ruby Harder heard an explosion. Same kind as the explosions my sister heard at the Town Hall."

"I'm not trying to prove anything, but think," Graves said. "Ruby Harder and her child were, presumably, asleep. Is she really sure that it was the sound of a bomb exploding that woke her? Or did she assume that 'must have been it' when she heard about the bombs at the Town Hall?"

"The bombs in Fletch Johnson's truck, parked out there?"

"No question in my mind that someone bombed the Town Hall to hide a murder, burn a body," Graves said. "But having done it, he finds another fire is aiding his cause. He's local, he knows local gossip. Nobody's going to be surprised to see him at a fire. And he, seeing Fletcher Johnson's truck, sees a way to frame a man who is a perfect suspect for that first fire. So you may have a client to defend if it turns out to be that way."

"Let me try something else on you," Uncle George said, and he sketched out Rich Nolan's theory about people with a past somewhere else, and at some other time. "He mentioned himself and you as two such people."

Graves nodded. "It's a clever idea," he said. "Dan Lewis comes to town, sees me on the street, and is reminded of some crime I committed some time in the past. He confronts me with it and I shoot him. I don't think it will hold water, George. Nolan's lived here for ten years, I for seven. I'm really Foster Graves. Nolan is really Rich Nolan. I can imagine a public figure like Dan Lewis coming to a strange town, being introduced to someone who calls himself John Jones and knowing instantly that he is really Tom Smith. That would call for an instant murder. It would explain what happened to the man in the Town Hall. He saw a John Jones wandering around whom he knew was really Tom Smith." Graves chuckled. "Of course, I'm inventing this because I really am Foster Graves, and Nolan has suggested it because he really is Rich Nolan. If there are twenty other people in town who came here from somewhere else, they could, I suppose, really be Tom Smith and not John Jones."

"You want me to take this seriously?" Uncle George asked.

"I want you to applaud my genius for inventing a first-rate mystery novel," Graves said.

"I applaud," Uncle George said, tapping his hands together. "But I'm not happy."

"Oh?"

"Because you've given me another trail I have to follow," Uncle George said. "Who is not who he says he is?"

"And three people who knew are dead," Graves said. "We know Dan Lewis, because of the nature of his business, could easily have spotted a John Jones-Tom Smith. How the Watson kid managed it will remain a mystery. But in the police lab is a jar of ashes, with a blob of melted lead in it, that was once a man—the first one to unmask a villain. If I were involved, George, my first concern would be to label that jar of ashes with a name."

"If no one comes forward to say that someone is missing we have no way to proceed. .Not even dental remains that could match a chart somewhere."

"A man isn't necessarily 'missing' if he's away from home

141

and hasn't checked in," Graves said. "He's on a business trip, a vacation, he has no immediate family to report to. So they read in the papers and hear and see on radio and TV that in the remote little village of Lakeview, a man was murdered and his body burned beyond recognition. The police haven't a clue as to who he was. You know how people are, George. 'It can't be anyone I know—that kind of thing doesn't happen in my world.'" Graves tossed away the stump of a cigar he'd been nursing. "Damn it, George, you've got a national network at your disposal with a show coming up at seven o'clock tonight that most of America will be waiting for. What really happened to their favorite commentator? So you ask for help. You've got Steve Whitmore, not unknown; you've got Laura Lewis—or whatever her stage name is—the glamorous, bereaved widow; you've got the police. The network should offer a substantial reward. Rich Nolan would probably contribute. You might come up with three genuinely missing men whom nobody had thought of as being missing. But that would eliminate the rest of the universe, wouldn't it? Believe me, George, the key to this case is the identity of that jar of ashes."

"It could work," Uncle George said.

"So get off your butt, friend, and start it rolling. You haven't got all day!" Graves grinned. "You've actually got less than half a day to get people lined up, appeals planned, money up front." He stood up and held out his hand. "And if you're still alive at the end of the day, drop by, dish the dirt, and I'll buy you a drink or three."

2

Still no sign of Joey anywhere. On his way back into town Uncle George stopped at Marilyn Stroud's cottage, looking for Ruby Harder. He explained to the girl about Joey and asked her to alert the young people she knew.

"They're all so involved in trying to find out what happened to Tiny Watson," she said.

"God help us, the same thing may be happening to Joey. It can't hurt them to keep an eye open for him." Uncle George started to leave and turned back. "I've just been talking to Foster Graves about the case, Ruby. He raised a question that's worth asking, I think. You told the police you heard the bomb that started the fire at your father's farm?"

She nodded.

"Did you hear it, Ruby? You and little Rod were asleep, nearly midnight. The question is, did you actually hear the bomb or did you just think you 'must have heard it' when you heard the talk about bombs?"

Ruby stared at him steadily for a moment. "To be honest, Mr. Crowder, I'm not sure. I know I woke up with a start—sitting straight up in bed. Some kind of noise had startled me awake. Then I saw the flames at the barn, heard my father shouting into the phone, and hurried to get Rod out of the house. I heard my father talking about a fire bomb to the first fireman who arrived and—well, yes, I guess I did assume that was what had waked me. So, later, I said I'd heard it. It's splitting hairs, Mr. Crowder, isn't it? I was wakened by a sound that I thought was a fire bomb exploding. The fire was going full force almost instantly, not like one that starts in a hayloft and spreads."

"If there wasn't a bomb—"

"Would it help Fletch?"

"The truth will help him," Uncle George said. "You heard a bomb, you heard what might have been a bomb, you assumed it was a bomb. Think about it and make sure, girl."

Back at the Inn, Uncle George talked to Babe Fallon and Whitmore about Foster Graves's suggestion. It seemed to him it took the two men forever to evaluate the idea, weigh the pros and cons, discuss whether it actually could be set up in time for tonight's broadcast. It was after two o'clock before they agreed to have a shot at it.

"Be here at six," Fallon told Uncle George. "Talk to your trooper friends—Purdy or Corbett, or both. I'll do what I can to persuade Laura. She's pretty nearly had it."

"A reward?" Uncle George asked.

"I'll talk to the network," Whitmore said.

"It shouldn't be chicken feed," Uncle George said. "Nolan might help if you ask him. After all, no one has to pay it if they don't get results."

"Where will you be if we need you?" Fallon asked.

A muscle rippled along the line of Uncle George's jaw. "I'm looking for my nephew who may have wandered down the wrong street," he said. "If I haven't found him, you may have to do without me."

As the afternoon wore on, Uncle George found himself thinking less and less about the planned broadcast, or the attempt to identify a "jar of ashes with a blob of lead in it." Joey's continued absence was becoming more than a cause for anxiety, it was downright scary.

"I find myself actually hoping he's had an accident some-where out there in the woods," Uncle George told his friend, Red Egan. "A fall, a broken ankle—something like that."

"So let's get serious about looking for him," Red said. "And we better do it before sundown."

"You can take the time?"

Red grinned at his friend. "It's part of the main case, isn't it—until it turns out to be a broken ankle."

The obvious starting point for a serious search was Rich Nolan's field above the old marble quarry, the last place

144

anyone had admitted seeing Joey. Rich Nolan had reported that Joey had headed down for the quarry after their conversation. There was no way of picking up a trail there. It hadn't rained for days and the hundreds of people who had walked over the territory had left it a mass of disturbed dry earth, with no very clear marks except the tire treads of the heavy crane that had pulled Dan Lewis's Mercedes out of the pool.

Uncle George glanced at the red setter lying on the front seat of his Jeep. "If I just had him to circulate," he said to Red Egan, "he could pick up Joey's trail in an instant."

"Can't walk at all?" Red asked.

"Not really. Not to circulate the way he would—if he could."

"They have a couple of pretty good dogs up at the trooper barracks," Red said. "Give 'em a whiff of some of Joey's clothes, shoes, and they could do a pretty good job. Better than nothing."

Uncle George hesitated. "Asking for some of Joey's things will throw a real scare into Esther," he said.

"You've got to tell her, sooner or later, that Joey's being gone is past thinking of as a game he's playing. I'll get the dogs, you get the clothes. I'll meet you back here."

It couldn't be ducked any longer.

Esther Trimble was in her kitchen when Uncle George got there. "Joey here?" he asked, hopefully.

"I don't know where he's gone to," Esther said. "Been gone all day. Didn't show up at lunchtime."

"There may be trouble, Es."

Esther put down the wooden spoon with which she'd been mixing something in a crockery bowl. "What kind of trouble, George?"

"I got a message from Joey earlier on that he was playing detective. Rich Nolan saw him out by the quarry this morning. Not a sign of him ever since."

"You and your damn fool games!" Hector Trimble had come through the connecting door to the pharmacy. "I saw your Jeep outside. Figured you'd had the decency to come and tell us where our boy is. I should have known something you taught him had got him into trouble."

"Every kid in town is playing detective today," Uncle George said.

"But Joey imagines you've made him an expert!"

"Dogs may be able to find him if he's hurt somewhere. I came here to get a pair of his shoes from you, Es," Uncle George said. "An undershirt or shirt that he's worn but that you haven't got around to washing yet—"

"That red mutt of yours going to play 'Find Joey' again?" Hector asked.

"Unfortunately not. Timmy's temporarily crippled. Red's getting a couple of trained police dogs from the barracks."

Esther had no questions. She left the two men to fetch what her brother wanted. Hector's face had turned from sardonic to genuinely alarmed. "The quarry pool," he said. "Can he have dived in there to look for something the troopers may have missed? He isn't all that great a swimmer, George."

"I hope to God not," Uncle George said.

Esther came back carrying a white plastic trash bag, which she handed to her brother. "A pair of shoes, pair of socks, and an undershirt. Will that do, George?"

"Perfect. Thanks."

"Should we come with you, George?"

"Stay here—in case Joey tries to reach you. The dogs will, or they won't."

Red Egan was already back at the quarry when Uncle George got there. He had two gray police dogs on chain leashes sitting beside him on a block of marble.

Uncle George glanced down at the quarry pool and made a diving gesture with his hand. "Hector suggests—"

146

"Let's pretend he didn't," Red said. He took the shoes, socks, and undershirt from Esther's plastic bag and presented them to the two dogs, who sniffed at them eagerly. Then he unhooked the leashes from their collars.

"Search!" he said.

The two dogs began to move around in widening circles, noses to the ground, tails erect and ramrod straight. Suddenly one of the dogs made a sharp barking sound and started down the crushed stone road to the main highway, his tail moving now. The other dog took up the trail behind him then, making on-the-trail sounds.

"Got it!" Red Egan said. He glanced at Uncle George. "Not in the pool, anyway."

The two dogs moved on down the road, working steadily. Being an expert with hunting dogs, Uncle George knew the trail was clear, no hesitation in the way either animal was working. They got to the foot of the road where it joined the main highway and the lead dog turned to the right, heading back toward town. Then he hesitated and began to yip. He'd lost it. He began to circle. The second dog acted the same way.

"If Joey walked out onto that macadam, would they still be able to follow?" Red Egan asked.

"Sun beating down on it all day, trucks and cars dragging hot rubber over it—trail would be intermittent at best," Uncle George said.

"And Joey could have hitchhiked a ride," Red said. "We can work both sides of the road, see if they can come up with it again. Which way? South toward town or north toward Mill River?"

"No way to guess. We'll have to try both ways."

"You taught him to play detective," Red said. "You ought to know how his mind works."

"You sound like Hector," Uncle George said.

"God forbid!"

147

Half an hour later the dogs had failed to find Joey's scent again.

"Most of the land on the other side of the road is Rich Nolan's," Red said. "I guess it would be all right if we set the dogs working over there."

"You start," Uncle George said. "I'll take a run up and tell him. The way things are here today, you see someone prowling your grounds you might not like it." He glanced at his wristwatch. "If Steve Whitmore got to him, Rich Nolan and his wife should be heading for the Inn pretty soon for the *Tonight Show*."

"You not going?" Red asked.

"Are you kidding?"

Uncle George climbed the rail fence and headed up across the adjoining field toward the Nolan house. Thirty years ago Pat Nolan had built this house with loving care, a concern for New England traditions, and lived there, hoping against hope that he would be united in the end with a son he'd never seen. Uncle George, drawing a will for him when his time came, received confidences from the old Irishman that perhaps no one else had ever had. There had been a love affair with a beautiful Irish girl named Maggie Flynn.

There wasn't any kind of a future for him in Ireland, so he left. Later he learned that he had a son, that the lady was bitter at being deserted, and she had married someone else and never wanted to see him again. Miraculously Pat became a multimillionaire. But all his money never found the girl for him again. Eventually he learned that she'd died giving birth to another man's son. His own son was somewhere in Ireland, growing up in some other man's home, presumably. Or perhaps he was living under the name of Richard or Dicky Flynn, his mother's maiden name.

The will was drawn. The only condition was that Richard should maintain this place in Lakeview that Pat loved so

148

dearly. The old man died, the will was probated, but Uncle George had had his trouble and left town. Executors of the estate hired a detective to go to Ireland to find Richard. He was deep in the Irish fighting, but it turned out he had a wife, Mildred. She was hard to convince, couldn't believe the incredible figures the detective quoted to her. In the end she was flown to America and to Lakeview to see for herself and listen to the bankers talk. It was real. And so she went back to Ireland, collected her husband, and came back to Lakeview to live the last ten years in luxury. Rich Nolan had taken his father's name in the process.

As he reached the crest of the hill, Uncle George looked down at the Nolan house and saw Rich and Mildred sitting on the flagstone terrace that overlooked the lake. They saw him coming as he approached, and Rich came to meet him.

"Mr. Crowder!"

Uncle George explained what he was doing there, asked permission to have the dogs try to find Joey's trail on this side of the road.

"But of course," Rich said.

"What could have happened to the boy?" Mildred asked, joining the two men.

"Maybe nothing but an accident," Uncle George said. "But after what happened to the Watson boy—"

"Do you have any idea what he was looking for? Rich told me he just wanted to have a look at where it all happened at the quarry."

"I know, Mrs. Nolan, but the reward is 'sugar plums dancing,' and kids have a way of thinking they may be smarter than their elders," Uncle George said. "Joey has been well trained in the woods. If he's had an accident, he'll know how to hang on until we find him. But if he really got onto something—" He glanced at his watch. "Aren't you two going down to be on the *Tonight Show?*"

"They asked us, but we preferred not to," Rich said.

"We'll contribute to any kind of reward they want to raise, but we don't want to go on camera."

"Be on everybody's sucker list in the world if we did," Mildred said.

"People will know you're putting up money—the Town Hall, the rewards," Uncle George said. "You'll be on sucker lists anyway."

"But if we stay off camera, we'll at least be able to walk down the street without people asking us for a handout," Mildred said. "You're not going to be on it either, are you? If you want to watch it from here when the time comes, you're welcome."

"Thanks. But if we haven't found Joey—" Uncle George pointed out to the field where the two police dogs were circling, wider and wider, searching for the scent of a boy that probably wasn't there. "It'll still be daylight when the show goes on, and Red and I will have to use every minute of it."

"Enjoy your company if you change your mind," Rich said.

"You'll hear your own ideas elaborated on by Steve Whitmore," Uncle George said.

"What ideas?" Mildred asked.

"Someone whose history is in another time, another place," Uncle George said.

"We've talked about it, love," Rich said to his wife. "I suggested to Mr. Crowder that the villain in our world is someone whose past isn't what it's advertised to be. The man in the Town Hall recognized him and died for it. Dan Lewis recognized him and died for it. I pointed to us and to Foster Graves as people who are thought of as local whose histories have no connection at all with Lakeview."

"And Graves agrees," Uncle George said. "But both of your histories are well known. Once again, Rich, Dan Lewis didn't say anything to you about the case that, in view of what happened to him, takes on more importance than it had at the time?"

Rich and Mildred exchanged glances. "Just nothing comes to the surface, Mr. Crowder," Rich said. "When we met the other time, almost eleven years ago, I was a hotheaded young rebel, fighting in the Irish Republican Army, named Dicky Flynn. Later the whole damn world learned that I was Pat Nolan's son and had inherited his fortune, taken his name. When Lewis came here on Wednesday, we talked briefly about the Irish politics of the time we first met, of the great fortune that came my way when my father's people found me. Lewis had a lot of things to do to get ready for his broadcast. He asked me to go on it with him—I'd agreed to rebuild the Town Hall—and I said no, for the same reasons I've given you for not going on tonight. We agreed to get together sometime before he left Lakeview and have a long chat about the old days and the present ugliness in town here."

"You knew him from that first meeting, Mrs. Nolan?" Uncle George asked.

"I didn't even know Rich, except by reputation, when that first meeting happened," Mildred said. "Rich and I got together later."

"And Lewis didn't say anything to you on Wednesday that suggested he was onto something?" Uncle George asked.

"Nothing," Rich said.

"As a matter of fact, we asked him that very thing," Mildred said. "He told us he didn't know any more than we did about what had happened here. 'Just beginning to feel my way,' is what he said."

"And felt his way right to the bottom of the quarry pool with a bullet in his head," Uncle George said. "Very soon after he talked to you, too."

"It still just doesn't make sense," Rich said.

"The *Tonight Show* may help to clear away some of the

151

fog," Uncle George said. "Thanks for letting us trespass. I wish I really thought it would produce results."

Babe Fallon, Steve Whitmore, and the network big shots did everything possible to make that *Tonight Show* memorable. They knew they might have their biggest audience ever, eager to hear news about the murder of Dan Lewis, a longtime favorite.

Not everything went exactly as they hoped. To begin with, the Nolans refused to appear on camera, although Rich had offered to contribute to the reward. The network chose not to accept that offer, preferring to make it all their operation. They offered $100,000 for information that would lead to the arrest and conviction of Dan Lewis's murderer. As the time for the broadcast approached, Fallon and Whitmore began to wonder if Uncle George would appear.

"It means he hasn't found the boy," Fallon said.

"And that means we may have another horror on our hands right in the middle of things," Whitmore said. "Dan Lewis is what this broadcast is supposed to be about."

"Heart of gold," Fallon said. "If something has happened to that boy, it means the killer is still just around the corner."

The two trooper captains, Purdy and Corbett, were ready.

"We should be out there doing something, but what?" Purdy said to Whitmore, just before air time.

The lobby of the Inn was crowded to its walls, just as it had been the night before. There were noticeably more strangers than there had been for that first broadcast after Lewis's murder. The whole area was wrapped up in Lakeview's horror, along with an army of reporters from everywhere.

"Five minutes to air time and counting," Babe Fallon

announced from the microphone on the camera platform.

The red eyes of the cameras began to blink and Whitmore took his place at the anchorman's podium. Fallon gave the "go" signal and Whitmore began.

"Good evening, ladies and gentlemen. This is Steve Whitmore, unhappily filling in for the late Dan Lewis. In the course of this day, those of you who are vitally interested have kept abreast of the news, and you know that nothing new has been added toward a solution to the tragic violences in this town of Lakeview. You know that since Dan's murder another victim has fallen to the killer, Mortimer Watson, a fifteen-year-old boy, shot by the same gun that was used to kill Dan. And now, as I talk to you, another young boy, Joey Trimble, is missing. He is being hunted for by his uncle, George Crowder, who was meant to be a guest on this show, and Sheriff Egan. These two men, along with two trained police dogs, are trying to pick up some trace of Joey, and we are all praying that there is, after all, no connection between this missing boy and a murderer who has already struck three times.

"This brings me to what we think is the main purpose of this broadcast tonight. I mention three murders, and I mean, of course, Dan Lewis's murder, and the killing of the Watson boy. But the third murder was the first. He is a man, still unidentified, whose body was burned to ashes in the fire at Lakeview's Town Hall in the early hours of Wednesday morning.

"George Crowder, unhappily not here while he searches for his missing nephew, is a onetime criminal lawyer and a student of crime. Crowder has come up with a theory that the police are inclined to buy. I wish Crowder was here to explain it to you, but I'm going to leave that to Captain Corbett, regional commander of the State Police."

Fallon adjusted a microphone over Captain Corbett's head where he sat just to Whitmore's right.

"One of the things that has blocked the police in their investigation so far," Corbett told the audience, "is the absence of motive. In the beginning there were the fires, and the burned remains of an unidentified man. At first it was thought that the fire at the Harder farm was the result of a quarrel between the farmer, Seth Harder, and a farmhand whom he'd fired, Fletcher Johnson. Revenge. But then, while that fire still blazed, the Lakeview Town Hall was struck by three fire bombs that completely destroyed it. In the ashes was found the burned skeleton of a man. In those ashes was found a blob of melted lead which we believe had been a bullet. And then Dan Lewis came here on Wednesday to do his *Tonight Show* here that night. During the afternoon, around three o'clock, he went to call on a Lakeview resident whom he'd met some years ago. He spent half an hour with Richard Nolan and his wife, said nothing to indicate that he had any special information about the case, and took off. His body was found about four hours later, a bullet in his brain, strapped in his car, submerged in an old marble quarry pool. That pool is less than a mile away from the Nolans' house, where Dan had been visiting. No one will admit having seen him after he left there.

"The night before Dan was killed, someone tried to set fire to George Crowder's house. It wasn't successful because a neighbor was close by and Crowder's dog tried to protect his master's property. The dog attacked the intruder and was shot in the shoulder. The neighbor stopped the fire before it got really started. The important fact is that ballistics shows that the bullet that was found in the dog was fired by the same gun that was used to murder Dan Lewis. And then on Thursday, the Watson boy was shot with the same gun. The murderer has neither left the area nor, apparently, tried to leave it. George Crowder has come up with an explanation for why the murderer is still here. I'm

154

going to let Captain Purdy tell you what that explanation is."

Captain Purdy took his place under the mike in the cameras' eyes. "Local people know George Crowder as a wise and respected neighbor, with a background in criminal law and the investigation of crimes. He was once our County Attorney here. According to George, the reason the murderer hasn't left town is because he is well known here and to disappear would be as good as a confession. But why was the man in the Town Hall killed? We believe that blob of lead in his ashes almost certainly was once a bullet fired from the murder weapon. There is no one missing from this area—except Joey Trimble—so we assume that the man in the Town Hall was not local. Dan Lewis was not local. But Tiny Watson was and so is the killer—local. What we have to assume, according to George Crowder, is that two strangers—the man in the Town Hall and Dan Lewis— saw somebody they've know from somewhere else, and know that he isn't the person he's been claiming to be here. As George puts it, 'A Tom Smith who is really a John Jones.' How the boy, Tiny Watson, came on that knowledge we can't guess. Or if Joey Trimble came on it, we don't know how. Dan Lewis, in his job, could very easily have seen a man he knew from somewhere else, operating under another name than the one he does here. The Watson boy and Joey Trimble, not so likely to know someone from somewhere else. But the man who became ashes in the Town Hall may be the key to the whole thing. If we could find out who he was, where he worked, who his friends were, we just might find out who is living here behind a false face."

"And so we come to the main purpose we have in mind for this broadcast," Steve Whitmore said, taking over. "The network is offering a reward of one hundred thousand dollars—let me say that over again—one hundred thousand

155

dollars, for information that will lead to the arrest and conviction of Dan Lewis's killer. One hundred thousand dollars! It is George Crowder's feeling that somewhere a man is missing . . . the man whose ashes were found in the Town Hall. He could only have been gone for three days so that family, friends, and business associates haven't suspected he is missing. On a vacation, on a business trip . . . no reason to check back with them. I'm sure that most of America is listening to us, or will hear about what we've had to say tonight. Somebody may say, 'Well, we haven't heard from Pete for three days. Let's check on him.' We feel if we could identify that man in the Town Hall, we might be on our way. If you could identify him for us, you might find yourself on the way to becoming one hundred thousand dollars richer. So . . . somewhere away from here someone is missing, and right here in town there may be someone who isn't who he claims to be. You have anything to add, Captain?"

Purdy spoke. "In a town like this, particularly in summer, there are people whose pedigrees aren't an open book. We are covering everyone, new property buyers, summer renters, transients we haven't bothered with because they can move on without attracting attention. God help us, this man hasn't moved on. He's stayed and killed. We need your help, folks, whether you get rich or not!"

Whitmore took over the mike again. "And now, ladies and gentlemen, I'd like to introduce a very brave lady who needs your help. She is known to you as Laura Stallings, a brilliant young actress, who in private life is . . . is the widow of Dan Lewis. Laura needs your help and has asked for this chance to speak to you."

Whitmore held out his hand. Laura Stallings came into the cameras' eyes. Blond, erect, with a kind of trained grace, she walked over to stand beside Whitmore behind the mike. It was hard to tell whether the almost deathly pallor was for real or a careful bit of stage makeup. Her fingers fastened in a tight grip on Whitmore's arm, and her dark eyes, wide and staring, looked around the audience as if she expected to see a villain there. She glanced at Whitmore.

"Thank you, Steve, for giving me this chance to ask for help," she said. Her voice was unsteady, but a controlled unsteady. She knew how to use the camera and suddenly her dark eyes were looking directly at every individual listener in America. "This is not the time to eulogize the man I . . . I've lost," she said. "Someday, someone more skilled than I will write about Dan Lewis, the reporter and commentator. Heaven knows he was one of the very best. But tonight I am talking about my husband, the man I loved, the man who loved me. He has been brutally, heartlessly murdered, an attempt made to hide his dead body in the cold waters of a marble quarry pool. There is a madman somewhere close by who has killed again since then, an innocent young boy. Another boy is missing. I beg you not to sit and watch what the police report, listen to what the commentators have to say. Be on the watch, be ready, to help us stop a madman from striking again. There is a money reward, I know, but your greatest reward can be that you have helped prevent a mad killer from taking another life, maybe someone close to you."

Laura Stallings-Lewis was silent for a moment, looking through the cameras into the eyes of her audience. The hands of the clock on the far wall moved close to the end of the broadcast time.

Laura Stallings's voice was unsteady yet commanding. "I need your help . . . help to find my husband's killer. Who saw Dan after he left the Nolans' place about three-thirty yesterday afternoon? A brief glimpse of him might tell us where he was headed. Who knows anything about the identity of the man who was murdered and left in the Town

Hall to burn? Who knows where poor young Tiny Watson was going when he was stopped and killed? Who knows anything about Joey Trimble, missing all of this day? Help in any one of these directions could be vital, because they are all part of a bloody pattern invented by a heartless killer. Please, please, help us!" The actress lowered her head and her lips trembled. "Please!"

The announcer came on for the sign-off.

It had been first a very interesting and finally a very moving half hour. It would be shown again later in the evening so that no one interested in the world beyond his nose would have failed to see it. Help should come from somewhere.

"That help should come from us," Captain Purdy said to Corbett when the crowd had thinned out of the Inn's lobby.

"Everyone is going to help, thanks to that Stallings doll . . . running around like chickens with their heads cut off," Corbett said. "The man we're after could be dying of laughter when he sees how futile all our efforts are."

"I was thinking while I listened," Purdy said. "I think what we have to do is start over at square one."

"Square one?"

"We've covered the town, we've talked to a thousand people, and we've come up empty," Purdy said. "We don't have one positive lead more than we had when it all began. We started out with Fletcher Johnson as an arsonist."

"Maybe he still is," Corbett said.

"He may have set the Harder fire, but he didn't fire bomb the Town Hall and he didn't try to torch George Crowder's cabin. We had him in custody when those things happened. He didn't kill Dan Lewis or the Watson kid. Same reason, we had him locked up. So I guess the answer is we have to start over at the beginning."

"The man who burned up in the Town Hall?" Corbett suggested.

Purdy nodded. "We don't think he was local, or he would have been reported missing by now. Who saw a stranger come into town? A bus driver? A hired taxi driver? Is there an unclaimed car in some parking lot or on a side street or backyard in the village? I suggest that's something you and a squad of men should start to work on, Captain."

"While you . . . ?"

"I'd like to make Dan Lewis my pigeon," Purdy said. "He was out around the back roads somewhere when he left the Nolans. I know everyone who lives out that way, I know who fishes and hunts out there. My territory. I like to think people will talk more easily to me than to a strange cop."

"Good old friendly Captain Purdy," Corbett said.

"I hope," Purdy said. "It's going to be dark in less than half an hour. Not much we can do visually, but we can talk to people."

The two trooper captains agreed on Purdy's suggested division of the work ahead. Corbett set out to find "square one" for the man who'd burned in the Town Hall—a bus driver, a taxi man, an abandoned car. A taxi would have come from out of town somewhere. A local man would have come forward long ago. The bus would also have come from out of town, but the same drivers covered the same route day after day. A stranger might have been noticed . . . coming from the north or the south?

Captain Purdy waited for Babe Fallon, producer of the *Tonight Show*, to wind up some details of the just-finished broadcast, and then flagged him down.

"I'm starting over from the very beginning, Fallon," Purdy said.

Fallon gave the trooper captain a blank look. Starting over from the very beginning after two days didn't speak well for trooper efficiency. Fallon had never heard Uncle

159

George describe Purdy as "super thorough." "Jim will turn over every stone along the way four or five times just to be sure he hasn't missed anything. Takes him longer than most, but you can be sure when he says there's nothing under that stone, there's nothing!"

"We may have missed something along the way," Purdy said to Fallon. "If I ask you questions I asked before, don't get impatient. We must have missed something because we've gotten nowhere."

Fallon nodded, his mouth moving in a twisted little smile. "My world for the last nine and a half years has come to an end with that broadcast," he said. "They won't call it the *Tonight Show* anymore . . . at least for a while. Memory of Dan. Ask away, Captain."

"Let's begin with Dan Lewis arriving in Lakeview," Purdy said. "That was . . . ?"

"About noon on Wednesday," Fallon said.

"The ashes were still hot where there'd been fires," Purdy said. "I'm not sure we knew then about the dead man in the Town Hall. Weren't you moving your operation from New York pretty fast—just to cover a couple of fires in a small town?"

"You have to understand our world and how it works, Captain. How it worked," Fallon added, bitterly. "Dan had been doing a series on terrorism, terrorism in many places. Suddenly over the news wire comes word of two fires here in Lakeview. Fire bombs! That didn't sound like an ordinary barn fire. More like big-league violence. Dan made a quick decision to come up here. It would hype up our series if we could broadcast right from the scene of the violence, talk to the people involved. Smart journalism, Captain."

"But no notion that it could be dangerous?"

"What reason was there to think so? It was over and done . . . we thought. By the time we got here, we heard that a man was burned to death in the Town Hall. In the beginning even that didn't seem to be part of the bombing—someone fell asleep in the building, a maintenance man trapped there after the bomb went off in the south wing. Reporters report what you cops dig up. We don't threaten anyone. We just report the news."

"So Dan Lewis got here around noon."

"Right. Driving his own car, the one he died in. My job was to set up the equipment for that night, check on the facilities at the Inn, set things up for a live audience. Dan's job was to circulate, talk to people, pick up some good guests to interview on the show—like you and George Crowder. It was almost as soon as Dan arrived that he heard that one Richard Nolan had offered to foot the bill for rebuilding the Town Hall.

"'I know that guy,' Dan told me. 'Long time ago, he was operating under the name of Dicky Flynn in Ireland, member of the IRA, right in the middle of violence over there. I was part of a team that went to Ireland to broadcast, actually interviewed Dicky Flynn. A little later there was another big story that I didn't cover. Dicky Flynn turned out to be the illegitimate son of a man named Pat Nolan, who had died and left Dicky a very, very rich man. He took his father's name, Nolan . . . Richard Nolan. He lives here, Babe!'"

"So he went to see him?"

Fallon nodded. "Make an ideal guest for that night's show, Dan thought. A man who'd lived by terror, knew the techniques, might be able to read something into what had happened here that you cops wouldn't see."

"And so he went out to Nolan's place to set that up," Purdy said.

Fallon's bitter smile reappeared. "Let's you and I stop right here, Captain," he said. "Dan told me that was what he was going to do when he left here. But I don't know, for a fact, that he did. I know Nolan says he did, but I don't know it. I never heard from Dan after he left here, never .

saw him again until I identified his body for your boys in the hospital morgue. You want something more than hearsay, Captain, your next stop is Nolan."

That was, in fact, the way Purdy wanted it to be. He didn't want a witness to tell him what he'd heard, just what he knew for a fact.

It was dark when Purdy parked his police car outside Rich Nolan's front door. The house was brightly lit, no question that there were people inside. The chiming doorbell brought a maid to the door. She was a local girl named Amy Parks.

"Oh, it's you, Captain Purdy!"

"Mr. Nolan at home?"

"Sure. Come in, Captain. I'll tell Mr. Nolan you're here."

She didn't have to. Nolan was already in the little entrance hall. "Recognized your car, Captain. Anything new?"

"Afraid not," Purdy said, "but I'd like to go over some old ground with you, if I could?"

"Come into the living room. Mildred's there. She'll be anxious to know what it's all about."

"And could help," Purdy said.

The captain still hadn't gotten used to seeing women in pants. He had to admit that Mildred's tailored slacks looked well on her.

"Any news of the Trimble boy?" she asked. "Mr. Crowder and the sheriff were out here looking for him. The police dogs didn't seem to be getting anywhere. Now that it's dark . . ."

"They don't need daylight to pick up a trail if it's there," Purdy said.

"Do they have any idea what could have happened to him?" Mildred asked.

"They hope it's an accident. Boy could have fallen somewhere, broken a leg or something, banged his head. Can't attract attention. If he can be found, George will find him."

"And if he can't?"

"I promise you one thing, Mrs. Nolan. If the same thing has happened to Joey Trimble as happened to Tiny Watson, George Crowder won't wait for the cops or the court to punish the man responsible. I'd rather face the Lord High Executioner than George Crowder in that situation."

"What can we do for you, Captain?" Rich Nolan asked.

"Tedious business," Purdy said. "I'm going back over ground I've already covered on the chance that something slid by me. Could we talk again about Dan Lewis's visit to you on Wednesday?"

"Of course."

"He got here—?"

"A little after three. Mildred and I were out on the terrace when his car drove up."

"And he left?"

"A little before four."

"You knew who he was when he got out of his car and came toward you?"

"We watch his show every weekday night," Mildred said. "He was as familiar as a member of your own family."

"I was really asking you, Mr. Nolan. You also knew he was a reporter who interviewed you ten or eleven years ago in Ireland?"

"No and yes," Rich said. "I never knew the names of the reporters who interviewed us back then. Different circumstances, different clothes, different thoughts running through your head. I've watched Dan Lewis's *Tonight Show* ever since we came to live here and I'd never connected him with that one afternoon in Ireland. He reminded me the moment he walked up on the terrace, and then, of course, it all came together. This sophisticated gent was the same dirty-faced, tired guy in work clothes who'd talked to me in Belfast long ago."

"So you rehashed those old days?"

163

"Not really very much," Nolan said. "He came up on the terrace, introduced himself, and of course Mildred and I knew who he was. But then he gave me a kind of amused little smile and asked if I remembered meeting him before . . . in a place called Hogan's Alley in the south of Dublin. So then, of course, it came back. That was a troubled time back there, we rebels in hiding, outnumbered, and the reporters had to make themselves look like something other than reporters to get to us. Dan Lewis had done a good job hiding his true identity that day, and when I began to see him regularly on TV, I didn't recall anything. He was that much different from the disguised man I'd talked to for fifteen minutes eleven years ago."

"So you talked about it?" Purdy persisted.

"Not really. He had only a little time to set up his show for that night. He wanted us on it. We wouldn't, and for the same reasons we wouldn't tonight. I agreed to tell him anything I could about terrorists and their techniques, but privately, not on the air. He asked if I could suggest anyone in Lakeview who might add to the show. I, of course, suggested you or someone representing the troopers, and I suggested George Crowder. And then Lewis left us."

"A few minutes before four, you say?"

"Yes. As I told you before . . ."

"Tell me again," Purdy said.

"We can't see the gates from the terrace, so Mildred and I didn't know which way he went," Nolan said. "If he went to the quarry, of course he went south."

"Why would he go to the quarry?" Purdy asked. "Nothing had happened there then."

"The quarry is a kind of showpiece in Lakeview," Mildred said. "Maybe somebody told him about a fabulous marble swimming pool out this way."

"Fallon tells me he was under pressure to get his show on," Purdy said. "He wanted you on it, which is why he

164

came here. He isn't likely to have gone sightseeing when he left here, or thought of going swimming. Did he ask you how to get to the quarry?"

"No, and I'd surely remember if he had."

"He didn't ask you how to get to any particular place or how to locate any particular person."

Nolan and his wife exchanged a glance. "He did ask about George Crowder, didn't he, Rich?" Mildred asked.

"Yes, he did, as a matter of fact. I told him that, after what had happened, Uncle George was likely to be almost anywhere except at his home—helping you, helping people who needed help. I did give him directions for getting to Crowder's cabin on the mountain. Obviously he didn't go there."

"Why do you say 'obviously'?" Purdy asked.

"Well, he went to the quarry!"

"Alive or dead?" Purdy asked. "Did he go there or was he taken?"

"In broad daylight!" Mildred said.

"I can't see what's in the trunk of a man's car no matter how bright the sun is shining," Purdy said. He was ready to go. "Lewis left here a little before four, you say. He was found in the quarry pool a few minutes after seven. That's three hours unaccounted for. You saw him go down your driveway, in his car, until the turn at the bottom took him out of sight?"

The Nolans nodded.

"One last question," Purdy said. "It would be fun someday to talk to you about the Irish trouble. But I think you did say that you were familiar with those Hitchcock fire bombs?"

"They're sold around the world to people who want to make trouble," Nolan said.

"You ever hear anyone in Lakeview mention fire bombs before they were used here?"

"No."

"Has anyone here in Lakeview shown a special interest in talking to you about your time in the Irish violence, want to pump you about your experiences?"

Husband and wife looked at each other.

"I can only think of one person, Captain," Nolan said. "I don't think it's what you're looking for."

"Name," Purdy said sharply.

"Joey Trimble," Nolan said. "It was a couple of years ago. I suppose he was ten or eleven years old. His Uncle George had been my father's lawyer, drew up the will under which I inherited. I suppose Crowder might know a great deal about those times in Ireland when my father was looking for me. He might have mentioned something about it to the boy, who came to me, hungry for an adventure story."

"It was just one afternoon, Captain . . . at least two years ago," Mildred said.

Purdy took a deep breath. "So, somewhere there must be a lead to what Lewis did from a few minutes to four on Wednesday afternoon until he was found shot and submerged in his car in the quarry pool around seven. But it doesn't seem to be here."

As Captain Purdy drove his car down the Nolans' driveway to the stone gates that marked the entrance, he saw the parking lights of a car stopped just south of the gates. As he slowed to make his turn toward town, the lights of the parked car came on bright, and then blinked on and off. Someone tapped on a car horn. Purdy turned his car so that his headlights focused on the parked vehicle and he saw that it was George Crowder's Jeep. Uncle George and Red Egan were standing just beside it, Uncle George reaching in to manipulate the lights.

"We saw you drive up there, Jim," Uncle George said. "Figured you weren't on your way to bum a double dry martini, so we decided to stay out of your hair. Anything new?"

"Nothing that moves us a foot ahead," Purdy said. One of the police dogs in the back of the Jeep, hearing a familiar voice, made a thumping noise with his tail. Purdy reached in to pet him and was greeted with a little burbling sound of pleasure. "Dogs didn't make it?"

Uncle George shook his head. "We've been over every inch of ground about four times," he said. "Same thing repeated. Joey came down the road from the quarry to the main highway, walked a few yards north toward town on the side of the road, and there it ends."

"He hitched a ride," Purdy said.

"Maybe," Uncle George said. "He's been warned about flagging down strangers, but if it was someone local, they'd know by now that we're looking for Joey and would have checked with us."

"A stranger just sees a nice-looking kid, offers a ride, doesn't know anything about what's going on here in Lakeview, and has no reason to report giving a kid a lift."

"Or if he was the villain of the piece," Red Egan said, "he could be planning to use Joey as a bargaining chip."

"Or if Joey saw something that tells a story," Uncle George said, "he could already have joined his friend, Tiny Watson."

"No point in being a pessimist, George," Purdy said.

"Why not, after what's happened here in the last forty-eight hours?" Uncle George said.

"Funny thing, George," Purdy said, "but Joey came up in my conversation with the Nolans. I was asking if anyone local had tried to pump the Nolans about the Irish violence, and the only person he could remember was Joey, a couple of years back."

Uncle George nodded slowly. "I seem to remember," he said. "Joey would have been eleven. Television news had

167

something about some bombing in Ireland. Joey asked me what they were fighting about. 'Get out from under the heel of the British tyrant,' I told him. He'd grown up on the heroic British Knights of the Round Table. Sherlock Holmes! I told him if he really wanted to know what it was all about he should ask Rich Nolan, who'd been a part of it till he came here to live."

"And Joey went to see Nolan?"

"Sure . . . I guess." Uncle George chuckled. "I remember he came back, puzzled, and asked me how you pick a side to be on when both sides are heroes."

"Nolan might remember what he really told him," Purdy said. "Could give you some kind of lead to what the boy was thinking about. Terrorism in his own backyard, he'd try to act like a British hero or an Irish hero."

"I think I'll run up and see what Rich Nolan remembers about the conversation with Joey," Uncle George said. "They weren't able to contribute anything to you?"

"I'm trying to account for the last three hours of Dan Lewis's existence—from four, when he left the Nolans', to seven, when he was found in the quarry. Nothing! No one saw him in town, no one saw him out here."

"Except the man who shot him," Red Egan said.

The two police dogs were transferred to Purdy's car, and Uncle George and Red Egan headed up the driveway to the Nolan house. Nolan didn't seem particularly glad to see them.

"We seem to have become some sort of special center of attention," he said. "Captain Purdy just left here."

"I know," Uncle George said. "We'd just finished working your fields with those police dogs. We saw Purdy coming out of your gates and flagged him down. The law seems to have come up empty in all directions. Red and I had no luck finding Joey, and Jim Purdy hasn't had any luck accounting for three critical hours on Wednesday afternoon."

"There isn't any reason, is there, that people should have been paying any particular attention to Dan Lewis during those three hours?" Nolan asked.

"You have to be kidding," Red Egan said. "A famous man, driving around our town in a flashy car. Not noticed?"

"I suppose. But maybe he wasn't driving around."

"He was trying to put a show together," Uncle George said. "That meant locating interesting people, like you, Nolan, who might act as guests. He wouldn't have been sitting by the roadside picking daisies."

"So how can I help you?" Nolan asked. He turned to welcome his wife who joined the men in the entrance hall. "It looks like more questions, luv."

"Mr. Crowder. Sheriff," Mildred said.

"I wouldn't bother you," Uncle George said, "except that Purdy told me about a conversation you had with Joey a couple of years ago. About the Irish rebellion, wasn't it?"

"Oh that," Nolan said. "What can that possibly have to do with what's happened here, yesterday and today?"

"Maybe nothing at all," Uncle George said, "but we're talking about a kid with a vivid imagination. A couple of years back he saw something on TV about the Irish troubles. Joey asked me what it was all about. I'm his expert on everything, you understand."

"'My Uncle George,'" Mildred said, with a faint smile.

"To tell you the truth, I've had enough problems with my own life, right here in Lakeview, to have interested myself in Irish problems. But I'd been your father's lawyer, Joey reminded me, I must have learned something about it from him. So I suggested that he ask you. You'd been right in the middle of it all, I told him."

"Well, he did come," Nolan said.

"With nine million questions," Mildred said, still smiling.

"You remember some of the questions?" Uncle George

asked. "Any details of the conversation? I remember Joey came home uncertain whether he should side with the brave Irish or the brave British."

Nolan frowned. "If you'd tell me what you're looking for, Mr. Crowder, it might make it a little easier."

"I'm trying to guess what Joey was thinking when he set out this morning," Uncle George said. "Terror strikes at his town, at his family—me! How did the brave Irish react to violence? You must have given him some examples, told him some techniques. Joey may be trying out one of those techniques for himself."

Nolan and Mildred exchanged glances again, and they were both smiling.

"I wish I knew how to take this seriously," Nolan said.

"The boy's been missing for almost twelve hours," Uncle George said.

"I didn't mean take his absence seriously," Nolan said. "That is serious and I wish I knew how to help. But that conversation we had two years ago . . . when he was eleven years old! It wasn't serious, Mr. Crowder. It was a kid asking someone to tell him a story and I told him one, about the brave Irish patriots fighting for their freedom against the powerful British Empire. I left out the real story of blood massacres, of bombings, of rape and arson. The Irish are my people and I made them look good, the British were my enemies and I made them look bad. But I just told the boy what I thought would entertain him, give him the exciting adventure story he was after."

"There was one thing I remember, Rich," Mildred said. "That just might . . ."

"Might what, Mrs. Nolan?" Uncle George asked.

"You mentioned 'techniques' for fighting violence," Mildred said. "I remember Rich telling the boy that the Irish were so often outnumbered . . . and we were! It was senseless to meet the enemy face to face when they might outnumber you five or ten to one. Rich said we just learned to hide in a hurry, and stay hidden until we could face the enemy on something like an equal footing. We might stay hidden for days, Rich told Joey."

"A thirteen-year-old boy would wonder how you arranged to feed yourselves," Uncle George said. "Joey missed both lunch and dinner today—if he's playing your Irish game."

Mildred's smile widened. "We told him we had caches of food hidden in prearranged hiding places. And we did, you know, Mr. Crowder. We'd just disappear off the face of the earth and wait for the odds to get more even."

Red Egan spoke for the first time. "You and Joey play hide-and-seek games, George. Joey hides, you send your dog, Timmy, to find him."

"But who would the boy be hiding from?" Nolan asked.

"Surely you don't have to ask that," Uncle George said. "Two fires, three murders, an attempt to burn me out. There's someone to hide from, God knows. If Joey thinks the killer suspects he knows something . . ."

"So he hitchhiked a ride from the quarry to somewhere and is hiding from the bad guy or guys," Red Egan said.

"He'd come looking for me, wouldn't he?" Uncle George asked.

"How do you know he hasn't?" Red asked. "You haven't been in any one place for five minutes all day. If he bought this idea of hiding, he wouldn't start looking for you until now."

"Why now?"

"For God's sake, George, it's dark. He can move around in the dark without the bad guy seeing him."

"Let's go take a quick look up at my cabin," Uncle George said.

"Let us know if you get wind of the boy, Crowder!" Nolan called after Uncle George as he and Red left.

There was no sign of Joey at the cabin, nor any sign that anyone else had been there. Uncle George carried Timmy, the setter, in from the Jeep, made a bed for him out of a couple of blankets, and applied the medication that Dr. Kellog had given him to the dog's wound.

"Kid could have found something to eat," Red said. "There are berries in the woods. He's an expert fisherman. And . . . and there's your refrigerator."

Uncle George took a quick look. As far as he could see, nothing had been touched, no bread cut from the loaf in the bread box, no sign that anyone had tried to cook anything.

"I've been wondering," Red said. "If someone wanted to burn you out, why have they left your cabin untouched all day?"

"Because the whole town is looking for someone to be somewhere they shouldn't be," Uncle George said. "Purdy's had a trooper checking out here every hour or so."

"So Joey hasn't been here, which means he's chosen some other place to hide," Red said. "You remember any special places when you were playing your games with him?"

Uncle George shook his head, slowly. "Those hide-and-seek games were for Timmy. Joey wanted to be found, left a trail Timmy could surely follow. No caves or rock hideouts where Timmy would fail." He took a deep breath. "I guess I'd better go report to Es and Hector that we haven't come up with anything."

"I wish we could come up with something that would get Esther off the hot seat," Red said.

"Damn it, Red, that hot seat's burning me quite a bit," Uncle George said. "Tiny Watson wasn't hiding, Red."

"But we found him," Red said. "Nobody's found Joey, which is at least something."

"Let's hope," Uncle George said.

The state of things in the town of Lakeview wasn't a surprise, but it was something to see. It was early evening, but not a house was dark. Apparently everyone was sticking to his own place of safety, neighbors not visiting, the local

172

movie house deserted in spite of offering a top-rated film. Part of the male population, those who were members of the volunteer fire company, and a few deputies signed on by Red Egan's office, were circulating, but in a kind of aimless fashion. They had no way to guess where terror might strike again. If there was no organized pattern to it, it could happen anywhere that wasn't carefully watched. Most people thought there was a pattern to it, a connection between arsons and murders, that no one had been able to put together yet.

Uncle George dropped Red Egan off at his office and headed across the village green to where his sister and brother-in-law lived. He dreaded the upcoming encounter. He knew Hector would blame him for Joey's disappearance, for putting himself in the path of danger, "playing games!" He knew Esther would be tortured by a pain that wouldn't go away unless or until Joey showed up again, all in one piece.

Hector was sitting in a wicker chair on the front porch when Uncle George drove his Jeep into the front yard. He didn't move or speak as Uncle George left the Jeep and walked toward him. A tight, bitter grimace showed under his clipped mustache.

"You're not dancing with joy, George," he said, finally, "so I guess I don't need to ask you."

"You know that if there was any sign of Joey, I'd have been here the instant it showed up. Where's Es?"

"Inside," Hector said. "Marilyn's with her."

Marilyn Stroud was Esther's best friend.

"Marilyn's mourning that Watson kid as though he was her own," Hector said.

"He was a kid in her school, someone she was helping to grow up," Uncle George said.

"Well, Joey is *our* kid. Es and I have a genuine reason for being scared for him."

"Yes, you do," Uncle George said. He hesitated, and

173

then he told Hector Rich Nolan's account of a long-ago conversation with Joey.

Anger clouded Hector's face. "What is there about that boy? All he does is collect heroes from people like you—Robin Hood, Sherlock Holmes, some Irish punk!"

"It isn't much to go on, Hector, but if he is playing some sort of game, he may be safer than we fear. I'll go in and report to Es."

As he started for the door, Hector called out to him. "Some guy been trying to reach you on the phone the last couple of hours."

"Who?"

"I don't know. Es got it written down inside."

"Why would anyone call me here?"

"Said your phone didn't answer. Knew Es is your sister. Said it was important."

In the house Esther and Marilyn were sitting in front of the stone fireplace. There had been a small log fire, but it had burned down to red coals. Esther was on her feet the minute Uncle George walked into the room.

"Nothing?" she asked.

"Sorry," Uncle George said. "A little guesswork." He repeated the Rich Nolan story.

Esther's face actually brightened. "It could be, George. I'd bought some ham for sandwiches at lunchtime. When I went to make them—before I knew Joey wasn't coming—I found most of the ham gone and a half a loaf of bread."

"Sounds hopeful," Uncle George said. "With your permission, I'll tan that kid's hide for not letting us know."

"Just get him home, George. I'll do the punishing."

"With a newly made apple pie," Marilyn said. "But that does sound hopeful, doesn't it, George?"

Uncle George nodded. No point in telling them that twelve or thirteen hours was a long time for a kid to play a game, and that a couple of ham sandwiches wasn't a normal supply of food for that length of time.

"Hector tells me somebody's been trying to reach me here on the phone."

"Oh, yes, George." Esther went over to the phone table and came back with a pad. "Derek Murphy, calling from New York City. Isn't that a familiar name, George?"

Uncle George looked straight past her at the wall beyond. "Too damn familiar," he said. "Eleven years ago . . ."

Esther remembered. "He was the lawyer for the defense in your case, wasn't he, George?"

"Your case" had been the time when George Crowder's world had fallen apart. He had been County Attorney, tried a man for murder, gotten a conviction, heard that his man had been executed by the state. It was after that execution that Derek Murphy had come up with evidence that proved a terrible miscarriage of justice had taken place. What could Derek Murphy possibly want eleven years later? His connection with Uncle George was long dead.

"He said it was very urgent, George."

"What can possibly be urgent between Murphy and me after eleven years?"

"He said it has something to do with what's going on here in Lakeview," Esther said.

"Somebody trying to get on the publicity train, I suppose," Uncle George said. "Will he call back?"

"He wants you to call him, collect if you like. But he won't be at this number until ten o'clock. That's a little more than an hour away." Esther tore the sheet on which the number was written off the pad and handed it to her brother. "Murphy lived somewhere near Hartford, didn't he?"

"New York City number," Uncle George said, folding the paper in half and slipping it in his pocket. "It isn't necessarily his phone. He could be staying there with someone."

Esther had already lost interest in Derek Murphy. "What do we do, George . . . about Joey?" she asked.

"If he's decided to play a game, be a hero, follow some

175

ground rules of his own, he may not be easy to find, Es, but he could be fine. We can tell him what we think of him when he gets back."

"And if that isn't the way it is?"

"Then, my dear sister, we're just going to have to play the cards as they're dealt to us. The whole town's got eyes open for him, and we can pray a little that he hasn't made himself dangerous to a killer."

He took Esther in his arms, held her very close for a moment, and then took off. The missing ham and bread was very little to base hopes on, but it was better than nothing.

One thing Uncle George had learned as a criminal lawyer, as a part-time crime fighter after his legal career had been terminated, as a hunter and fisherman—don't overestimate your endurance. You can go without sleep for a stretch, but only so far. The time had come to take time out to refresh. Back at his cabin, he called Red Egan's office and the State Police barracks to report where he could be found. Then, as he took off his jacket, he touched the paper on which Esther had written Derek Murphy's telephone number in New York.

Murphy and Uncle George, beyond their courtroom encounter, had not been personal friends. Uncle George had respected Murphy as a lawyer, and if the outcome of their court battle hadn't been so tragic, they might have found themselves friendly contestants in the courts over the years. Uncle George couldn't imagine what Murphy might have that would have any bearing on the Lakeview situation. But they were so far out at sea, it would be foolish not to find out what Murphy had on his mind. A quarter to ten . . . Uncle George switched on his television set to kill those fifteen minutes. There was the same rehash of facts he already had, but for want of hard news, the network was giving half its time to a revolution in Central America, and the bribery trial of a federal judge somewhere in the Midwest.

At precisely ten o'clock Uncle George dialed the number Esther had written on her slip of paper.

A man answered on the first ring.

"Derek Murphy here."

"Murphy? This is George Crowder. You left a message with my sister."

"Thanks for calling," Murphy said. "However, you may be the one saying thank you before we're finished."

"Esther says you told her you had something of interest about the case up here."

"Interest is putting it mildly," Murphy said. "Look Crowder, we both had an unhappy experience together. You convicted the wrong man, working with what the police gave you. I lost a client who didn't deserve to die . . . because I was too slow finding facts that would have saved him. You were eventually booby-trapped by those facts, but I always thought you did a fine job as a lawyer. It was the cops who blew it."

"Thanks."

"I've been sitting around here, listening to and watching the news, and I suddenly realized you were about to be booby-trapped again. Since I knew it, I found I wanted to warn you."

"You know that I don't know what you're talking about," Uncle George said.

"One of the key figures in what's happening up there in Lakeview is a man named Rich Nolan, who once operated in Ireland under the name of Dicky Flynn," Murphy said.

"True. Rich is Pat Nolan's son. Pat was a client of mine . . . before our trouble, Murphy. I drew Pat's will by which his illegitimate son, Dicky Flynn, inherited umpteen million dollars."

"And the son was your client when he came forward to collect?"

"No. You and I had our thing together between the time

177

Pat Nolan's will was drawn and his death. I stopped practicing law after our disaster and left town. Another legal firm took care of Pat's affairs when he died, located his son, brought him over from Ireland to collect. Rich has lived here ever since. Married, no kids."

"And he's going to rebuild your Town Hall, has offered a reward for the arrest and conviction of the killer?"

"That's right."

"Are you sitting down, Crowder?"

"You mean the big news is coming?"

"That's what I mean," Murphy said. He spoke slowly and very precisely. "The man living in your town as Rich Nolan is not, and never was, Pat Nolan's illegitimate son. I'm glad to hear you aren't the person who vouched for him. He is not and never was Dicky Flynn."

"Now hold on just a minute," Uncle George said. "He produced all the documentation necessary to satisfy Pat Nolan's lawyers. He has a wife who vouched for him. They've lived here quietly and peacefully for ten years. Of course he's Dicky Flynn. He took his father's name after Pat died."

"Dicky Flynn has been dead for more than ten years," Murphy said.

"Oh, come off it!" And then Uncle George remembered that somewhere along the way he'd heard that Dicky Flynn was dead. "The announcement of the death of rebels was and is a common thing," he said. "I remember Rich told me some years ago that it was a way to make an escape easier. If it were announced that a rebel leader was dead, the British would stop looking for him. He told me he was 'dead.' It was the only way he could get out of Ireland and come to America to claim his inheritance."

"I know Dicky Flynn is long dead," Murphy said, in a hard, cold voice. "I know because he died in my arms. My clothes were soaked with his blood. A shot-out in the back alleys of Belfast."

178

Uncle George was silent for a moment, every muscle in his body was tense.

"You still there, Crowder?" Murphy's voice came from New York.

"Yes, I'm here. Tell me, if what you say is true and you've known it from the very first, why didn't you expose the imposter when he stepped forward to claim Pat's estate?"

"Because I was still in Ireland, fighting for my life," Murphy said. "We didn't read American newspapers, didn't watch American TV. We weren't interested in a rich American leaving a fortune to a long-lost son. I just didn't know about it until it was all revived in the last couple of days. But somebody did know, and it cost him."

"Somebody?"

"The man whose body was found in the Town Hall up there. I'd bet my life that he was someone who stumbled on the truth, went up to Lakeview to put the blackmail bite on this fake Nolan, and paid for it."

Again silence in which only the sound of men's breathing came over the wires.

"If this is true," Uncle George said, finally, "then we know what happened to Dan Lewis. He went out to the Nolans to talk to a man he'd interviewed ten years ago in Ireland, and the man he saw wasn't the man he remembered."

"No question," Murphy said. "I called you because it's such a wild story and I knew you'd listen. The cops would probably laugh at me. I didn't want to see you behind the eight ball again. But I'll come up there, confront this dangerous bastard, expose him. But I hope for a little protection in the process. This fake Nolan doesn't even stop at children. You found your nephew yet?"

"No, and you haven't made me hopeful. How soon can you leave New York?"

"First thing in the morning. Leave here at seven, be up there by nine-thirty."

"I'll meet you at the State Trooper barracks," Uncle George said. "Meanwhile, I suggest you don't talk to reporters—or anyone. Nolan won't leave town. He has no reason to at the moment."

Uncle George was silent for a moment, staring down at his hands, which he was flexing and unflexing.

"Rich won't ever have any reason to leave town," a thin, cold voice said from behind him. Uncle George spun around. Mildred Nolan was there, holding a revolver in both hands, stretched out in front of her and pointed straight at Uncle George's chest. "Neither you nor your talkative friend are ever going to have a chance to tell what you think you know—to anyone!"

A gun in the hands of a person who has already killed is far more dangerous than one in the hands of someone who is thinking of pulling that trigger for the first time. Mildred Nolan, or whatever her name was, faced him, solid as a block of ice. She wasn't thinking about what would happen if she pulled the trigger. She knew. The man in the Town Hall was dead, Dan Lewis was dead, Tiny Watson was dead, and . . . and Joey? Uncle George told himself he had to stay in one piece just long enough to make some kind of deal for Joey—if it wasn't already too late.

The woman was across the room, ten or twelve feet away from Uncle George. There was no way he could make some kind of quick move to disarm her. She could empty the six shots her gun held into his gut before he could lay a hand on her.

"You seem to have known my friend was going to call me," Uncle George said, in a perfectly normal voice.

"I knew," Mildred said. "I also knew that he couldn't call you between eight and ten. He was involved in a TV show, a two-hour special . . . nothing to do with the situation here."

180

"So why did you wait so long to get here?"

"Because I didn't know till half an hour ago that you and Murphy were going to get together. My man in New York just came on the information by luck."

"Someone else you'll have to eliminate?"

"Someone else?"

"The one who told you I was about to get dangerous information from Derek Murphy. When you've killed me, then he's got you over a barrel, doesn't he?"

Mildred gave him a short, mirthless chuckle. "You think I'd put my life in the hands of a man whose tongue I couldn't control?"

"There are a lot of questions I'd like to ask you, Mildred, but I'm afraid you aren't going to give me time. But there is one that's important, life and death as far as I'm concerned."

"I know," Mildred said. "Where is your blessed nephew?"

"And?"

"Would you believe that I haven't the faintest idea?" Mildred said. "Now don't get itchy! Just stay still, Crowder."

"I'm not moving, Mildred."

"All the things you've got on my list of crimes, the one that doesn't belong there is your nephew's disappearance. I haven't the remotest idea what's happened to your precious Joey." She took one hand off the gun and flexed her fingers. Uncle George moved, a small reflex move, but he saw that she was still in full control. "When Rich and I were fighting the British in Ireland," Mildred said, "I could shoot the eye out of a sparrow with either hand. I can still do it, Crowder."

"When you're about to hear the referee count you out," Uncle George said, "the strangest thoughts pass by you. I found myself thinking of my sister, Esther. Her testimony is interesting, isn't it. She saw a small, dark-haired boy running from the south wing of the Town hall after the third fire bomb went off—small, lithe, agile, dark hair worn down to the nape of his neck. I look at you, Mildred, wearing those tailored slacks, that dark blue shirt, your hair worn short for a girl but long for a boy, and I realize Esther got her sexes mixed up. She saw a girl, not a boy. It was you, wasn't it, Mildred?"

Mildred gave him a tight-lipped smile. "Your sister's testimony will stand, Crowder. You aren't going to be able to cue her in."

"I guess I'm not going to be able to do much of anything, am I?" Uncle George said. "So satisfy one bit of curiosity before you pull that trigger, lady. Who the hell are you?"

Her tight little smile froze. "I am Mildred Flynn, wife of Dicky Flynn."

"Who died more than ten years ago?"

"Right. I am Dicky Flynn's widow."

"And who is this phony you've been passing off as Dicky Flynn-Rich Nolan?"

"My brother, Archie Fowler," Mildred said. "Oh, you drew a tight will for Dicky's father, old Pat. Almost a billion dollars to go to Dicky, no strings attached. But if Dicky didn't claim it, did his widow have a chance? Thanks to you, Crowder, she did not. All that money would have gone to an animal hospital, and a cure for gout, which old Pat had." Mildred's voice was bitter. "So I came over here to see what the situation was, realized no one could possibly identify Dicky if he was still alive to be seen. I had all his records, his birth certificate, his medical history, and three years of living with him. Archie was willing to share those millions of dollars with me, and it worked. It's worked without a hitch for almost ten years. And then, three days ago, a black-hearted Irish creep walked into our living room and threw the book at us. He knew Archie wasn't Dicky or

182

Rich. It was shell out. I chose 'shell in,' right between his greedy eyes. We had to get rid of his body. We had to make sure no one knew he'd ever existed. Archie suggested fire, and a way to use it. He set fire to the Harder farm, which borders our property to the north. That brought all the people from town out here. I drove our dead man into town. The Town Hall would be a perfect funeral pyre for him—no one there. We had the fire bombs. Brought them from Ireland with us years ago."

Talking seemed to relieve unbearable tensions. Getting it all out somehow helped her. But Uncle George knew that the more she revealed, the less chance he had of escaping her next murder.

"It all worked fine until Wednesday, when Dan Lewis walked into our house, took one look at Archie, and knew he wasn't Dicky or Rich. Left me no choice." She looked down at her gun. "The eye of a sparrow," she murmured.

Keep her talking!

"What about Tiny Watson?" Uncle George asked.

"Damn little fool! Archie and I had to talk. It wasn't safe to talk with Amy Parks, our maid there, the cook. So we went out to the summer house in the garden. I guess what we talked about was enough to hang both of us. Talked about, among other things, taking another shot at this cabin. My first try had been aborted by Bob Reed and your dog. While we were talking someone sneezed—right behind us! Tiny Watson had been there all the time, listening!"

"The eye of the sparrow," Uncle George said, after a moment.

Mildred nodded. "When it gets started it stays started. We'd hoped to distract you, Crowder, but you got in deeper and deeper. We'd tried to frame your client, Fletcher Johnson, but you didn't buy it." She took a deep breath. "And now, Crowder . . ."

183

The sharp crack of a rifle shot split the night. Mildred screamed, dropped her revolver, and bent double, clutching a shattered hand. Uncle George made a dive for the revolver before he saw where the rifle shot had come from.

Then he saw, standing in the doorway from the kitchen, his face the color of ashes, clutching a rifle in hands that were marble white, his nephew, Joey Trimble.

"I'm sorry I took so long, Uncle George," the boy said in a shaken voice. "I couldn't get my hands steady enough, and there'd only be one chance. If I missed . . ."

Mildred was on the floor, writhing in her own blood. Uncle George took the boy in his arms and held him very close.

"Perfect timing, Joey," he said. "I'm going to call the troopers, and then you get on the phone to your mom."

The arrest of Mildred Flynn for three murders, arson, and the plan to murder George Crowder wasn't to become public knowledge till days later when the grand jury brought in indictments.

The final piece of the Lakeview story on that final night was Joey Trimble's big moment. He had been playing a game, but very real to him.

"I remembered your telling me, Uncle George, that when you saw a certain kind of action was needed you didn't tell anyone, because it might leak and destroy your whole purpose."

The boy, his parents, Uncle George, and Sheriff Red Egan were sitting in the Trimbles' living room as the boy talked.

"Someone had tried to set fire to your place, Uncle George, and I saw no one was covering for you afterwards. They could come back, burn your house, destroy your guns and fishing equipment. So I decided to cover."

"Without telling us!" Hector said.

"I couldn't tell you and Mom, Dad," the boy said. "You might have let it slip somehow, and it would have spoiled everything."

"Thanks for your confidence," Hector said.

"Anyway, nobody came all day, all afternoon, right into darkness. I'd borrowed one of your rifles, Uncle George— the Winchester you taught me how to use." His lips twitched. "I owe you a can of soup. I got awfully hungry along the way. But I did clean up the pan and the soup bowl."

"You did fine, boy."

"Well, just when I was ready to give up, you came home, Uncle George. I was about to tell you that I'd been there all day, protecting your property, but you were on the phone. And then I saw Mrs. Nolan coming up the drive. That didn't bother me. She was, I thought, a friend." The corner of Joey's mouth twitched. "Then she did a funny thing. She didn't go to the front door and knock or just walk in. She went to the back door . . . to the place where the person who set fire to your place went, Uncle George. There's still a pane of glass missing there, where the first person reached inside to open the door and got himself—herself, I guess—attacked by Timmy. That's what Mrs. Nolan did now. She knew exactly where to go, reached in through the broken pane, and unlocked the back door. That looked real crazy to me, so I watched. When she went through to your front room, Uncle George, I went around to the side and looked in. There she was, holding a gun on you! Well, I tried to take aim at her with the Winchester, but my hands were so shaky I was afraid to try anything. If she'd just keep talking!"

"You heard what she was saying?" Red Egan asked.

"Every word, and that made me even more scared, because I knew she was a killer."

"Why did you have to shoot her in the hand?" Hector

185

asked. "You could have shot her in the back. You couldn't miss that size target, even with shaky hands, could you?"

"She was pointing her revolver right at Uncle George," Joey said. "If I shot her in the back, her finger might have squeezed the trigger . . . just a sort of reflex. So I waited, trying to get steady, and I realized she wasn't going to talk anymore. It was then, or never. So . . . so I fired."

"Crazy kid!" Hector said.

Uncle George put his arm around Joey's shoulder and gave him a hug. "Stay that crazy, Joey, for as long as you live," he said.